BIG CITY

BIG CITY

MARREAM KROLLOS

FC2

TUSCALOOSA

Copyright © 2018 by Marream Krollos
The University of Alabama Press
Tuscaloosa, Alabama 35487-0380
All rights reserved

FC2 is an imprint of The University of Alabama Press
Inquiries about reproducing material from this work should be addressed to
The University of Alabama Press

Book Design: Publications Unit, Department of English, Illinois State
   University; Director: Steve Halle, Production Intern: Jennifer Glasscock
Cover Design: Lou Robinson
Typefaces: Knockout, Adobe Garamond Pro, and Avenir

Library of Congress Cataloging-in-Publication Data
Names: Krollos, Marream, 1976- author.
Title: Big city / Marream Krollos.
Description: Tuscaloosa : FC2, 2018. | Based on the author's thesis
   (doctoral)—University of Denver, 2011.
Identifiers: LCCN 2018004909 (print) | LCCN 2018010230 (ebook) | ISBN
   9781573668781 (e-book) | ISBN 9781573660679 (pbk.)
Classification: LCC PS3611.R646 (ebook) | LCC PS3611.R646 B54 2018 (print) |
   DDC 813/.6—dc23
LC record available at https://lccn.loc.gov/2018004909

The author wishes to thank Joanna Ruocco and the editors of *Birkensnake*
for the publication of "Hushed."

BIG CITY

THERE ARE HORSES AND LIGHTS IN THE CITY

If you were above the city you would see the lights. From above the clouds above the city the lights of the city are blurred. The clouds cover the city. The lights are under water. It could all be Atlantis. What an unnatural beauty the city is. Blue, yellow, red lights are a city from above that looks like crystal jewelry you can hand to a friend. If you want to see a cross you can stare at the lights and you can see that within the lights there are lights in the shape of a cross. It can mean nothing. It can mean someone has sacrificed something for you in this city. A man who does not have a house or a car stumbles around to remind the people of the city why they must wake up early in the morning. On the streets of the city there are horses. They travel with blinders on, in and through the lights of the streets of the city. The people of the city take away the horses' peripheral vision. If the horses saw all the lights they might be frightened. You think this life is so cruel I can want something I will never have. In a car in the city the man sitting next to you feels like a friend, but he won't tell you why he has come. This hurts you enough to have to pretend he has come to the city to meet a mistress. He is too ashamed to tell you. His shame makes your shame better. There must be a reason why the people in the city need the horses. There must be a god who loves the horses. The people of the city must not frighten the horses. Clouds look like something that could be scooped up in your hands, something you can fall on. Everything has been the same since you realized you would fall in and through clouds. You should be able to take off these scabs on your face with your nails. You should find perfect skin beneath the scabs you can scrape off with a nail. First there is blood, then another scab again if you wait. If you wait, a scar. Everything is the same. Even skin does not do what you can see in front of you. Even skin has a punishing system. Looking down from above the clouds look like mountains, valleys, fields made of the gushing milk of an animal whose baby has been plucked away. If you tried to walk on them you would fall right through. What looks the softest can disappoint you. The horses can only see what is in front of them. One car. One man. One house. Life is so cruel you can want things you can't have. You should be able to, if you feel a gushing in your chest while talking to a friend, grab a face and kiss on the mouth. But that is not what friends do. You find something to stuff between your legs without realizing it. Walking in the city you do not realize what you look like. You don't know what you look like when you speak. Until the people of the city remind you, you are speaking loudly. When you begin to think about your voice you can imagine it. The parts of you that are too short, too long, too thick, too small. You cannot be a natural beauty. What you would have said changes. The horses can focus. They will not be disturbed by their vision. I am too loud when I speak. We are also too loud. The horses stay quiet in the city. I can tell you what we feel sometimes. A single thin needle pressed into our foreheads. A needle pressed through the bone of our chest punctures the skin of our lungs. We can sleep with closed eyes pressed tightly. Open eyes only pretending not to feel like pin cushions when they open up early in the morning. As if life cannot be so cruel you can want things that don't exist. A house, a car, a man, god. I am fine. God. I am shamed. In front of the people of the city I spoke too loudly. Can you hear me over the noise of the city? I have said many words too loudly before. Only the horses can see me. That is why when I wake up I can feel the thick black cloud that moves in my stomach. There is nothing you can say to make people in the city love us. Then what good is it. To speak at all. To walk out into a street to be with the horses.

Some people in the city are alone in their beds.

It's hard to start out here. It is not just him. It's just hard to start out. Everybody wants to be something here. It's hard to start out. They are all only putting their fingers inside their mouths and biting down just to feel something.

People in the city are alone in their beds.

She told the class that mothers kill their children more than any other kind of people kill children. What's that supposed to mean? It is too harsh to mention these things. It's too hard hearted. The simple logic is that they have easy access to children. It's not that bad really. It's only because they have access to their children. She wanted to make it sound so bad. So bad. Don't be so sensitive. Don't be so sensitive. When people aren't around children, they don't kill them.

People in the city are alone in their beds.

It doesn't matter if she misses you. It is just a feeling. She may miss you, but she won't do anything about it. You think if she misses you enough she will call you, but that is not true. If she feels guilty enough, misses you enough, she may change, become a better or worse person than she was with you, but she will still forget about you. That's how it works. That's just how it is. That's what you do too. You regret what went wrong with a person, and so try to be different with the next person, but you don't call the person you wronged to apologize and try to make things work. You know everything is already poisoned.

People in the city are alone in their beds.

It's just how they sweet-talk you, tell you what you want to hear, things that make you feel good. Then they take the feeling away from you when they stop paying attention to you, and you want to hear those words again. It's not even that man you want anymore. You feel it was never real, that you never were good enough for it in the first place, stupid to have believed it, but you want to believe it was real, and only he can make you feel it was real by paying attention to you again. Then when he says something to make you feel good again, you have him, you are happy to have him again, then he takes it away by not paying attention to you, and you have to stick around until he gives it back to you, again. He builds you up, then breaks you down. You can't believe you let him stare at you naked in sunlight. You were basically saying see, here are the little hairs I missed on my legs. Here are the bumps from the ingrown hairs on my thigh. These stains on my stomach are marks left over from scabs. These here are the marks left from when my stretched out skin would not come back to where it was. You are not now what you were before. No wonder he said nothing.

People in the city are alone in their beds.

When he feels she wants him he is happy. He feels energetic and excited and everything goes well for him that day. Then when she doesn't want him he feels sick, nauseated, tense. He thinks cleverly to himself the opposite of being desired is the desire to vomit, or because not being desired leads to the desire to vomit. Either way it is just a physical feeling, like having a fever. It will be over and done with soon enough. It will go away just like an illness goes away always, after it takes its course. What doesn't kill you . . . How could he die from this? He could change, for the worse, maybe, but . . . No, every time one of them stops wanting him he feels like this. But the sick feeling has always gone away. Every feeling eventually goes away.

People in the city are alone in their beds.

She used to heal so much more quickly. She used to give herself these scabs on her face and have perfect skin underneath them in a week or so. It's as if her skin isn't moving anymore, not like it used to. The older she gets the more slowly her skin moves. Her cells stop moving and stand still on top of each other. She can't heal as well if the new skin isn't pushing and fighting to take over the broken skin. There are too many still cells on her face. She hurts her skin now and it stays hurt. It stays the same skin she has hurt. It stays where it is, what it was. She has to start using thin needles to get to the ingrown hairs. She has to stop scratching at the skin of her face. A thin needle could easily get under her skin.

people in the city are alone in their beds

if there are men watching him from those windows

if they are taking pictures of him

if they are trying to make him look better by keeping the camera at certain angles because they know it would hurt him if they took pictures of him naked in bed with his gut looking like this

if they want him to look good in pictures because they think he does

if the pictures end up somewhere where other men can see them and if they all think he looks good too

if somebody is watching

People in the city are alone in their beds.

She used to actually say a little prayer every time she heard sirens at night in this city. She would pray for whoever might be bleeding. Now every time she hears sirens she wonders how much can naturally leave the body at the same time. Shit and piss and blood and milk and mucus and saliva and tears can all leave at the same time. A woman sitting on the toilet naked, crying, spotting, and lactating at the same time? Yes, maybe. Not likely, but maybe. There is a woman who is crying while she's shitting and pissing and she's bleeding and there's mucus and spit all over her face and her breasts are dripping milk onto her fat gut. Men have neither, do they? Men do not have blood or milk. What else can leave the body? Yes, she remembers.

If only she knew what would happen when she died, no matter what it is that could happen. She would know how to live life. She would know what is right and wrong to do while she is alive. She would know what to feel about life. If only she knew what happened when we died.

A MAN IN THE CITY IS WRITING A STORY ON A BUS

He thinks to himself, the sight of the nape of this man's neck is the only comfort I have here.

Is she a man or a woman?

Everybody is against me.

Why should his kisses redeem her? It is the skin on her stomach that was wrong to stretch out over so much fat tissue, when touched by the skin of this man's lips, nothing happens. It is not removed. It is not punished.

What is wrong is the feeling I have. Different thoughts are spinning around my head all the time. Then, suddenly, some of them stop. Some of them are bad and some of them are good. If only the happy ones keep swirling, then I am happy. If the bad ones keep swirling, then I am sad. That's what makes my moods. Thoughts like those bugs who light up at night and twirl around trees. Some of them light up, some of them turn off. Everybody is against me. I see only the streaks of lighting they fire off towards me. The place where my heart is goes murmuring. It is not painful, it is uncomfortable. This is where your heart is, it says to me. What is this fighting and why does it happen? What are expectations and why do they come with contact? She did not have a pure feeling of love for me. I know the signs. One woman is walking past me. If she stops to look at me, and smiles, that is good. If she looks at me a certain way, this feeling will stop. It will stop if she wants to speak to me. The signs are expectations too. Everybody is against me. I can try to fight them, but there are too many. Whatever is blood for them they will take from me. Even things can be blood. My feet I accept, however. The hair can be removed there and they will look strong. Only one foot has scars from bites. My legs are good from the knee down, strong and firm. Except for one ankle where there are scars from bites. My thighs are not scarred, but the skin of my thighs is flimsy from having stretched out over too much fat tissue. Hairs are all over my thighs.

Stretch marks wrap around her thighs. She is a woman.

The skin of my ass is not smooth, but hairy. The small of my back is filled with little hairs and bites. The rest of my back has bites and purple marks. My stomach has hair and three scars from hairs who keep growing under the skin. My arms dangle and are scarred. My face has scars. I pick at the skin. I write on my face the home I have had, then, I want to wash it and be new and young again. A sign. A man says may I sit here. He does not talk to me. Expectations. I always drink too much like this. I always want it, but I can never enjoy it. That is need.

A man says to her I will draw on you in your own home. To give tattoos. She wants to say yes, but it is too easy. He may touch her with his hands not just his needles. Then I will be wrong. Something will happen to the skin he kisses. He may ask her who wrote this, as he is touching her skin.

There are scars on the sides of both my wrists. The veins on my hands burst out of thin skin.

Do you want to know what I would look like if I were a man, she asks him sincerely or sweetly. She asks him. She asks him pleadingly.

If I were a man?

I loved and hated her at the same time. I feel two things always. Every time I do something it is not right. I do another thing. It is not right. I expect things to be this way. I expect to be wrong. I don't know how to be right, instead of wrong.

So, she wants to be right to only a person. One person. Who will not stare too long, or too briefly. A person. To be poetic I will say a place. She will try to be right to a plum.

The only way to live is to know that I am wrong. That is comfort because it is knowledge.

The sun stares at me too long sometimes she says. Angrily. Childishly. In a child-like tone. Like a child. She says.

I will do this because ink is a poison I cannot eat, and paper is made of wood. I stain wood with this poison. Poison moves on wood to make shapes and patterns. The shapes are the bad feeling. They are all against me. Are they all well loved? Every time I have felt loved there was a light. Light is good. Dark is bad. Dark needs light and light needs dark. I cannot write with black ink on black paper. I cannot see the poison. It needs the friction. Ask me, man. Ask me. Who wrote this? I did.

I did.

A homeless man who I give money to hugged me. If he hugs me every time I see him from now on, that is a sign. A homeless man who has just been released from prison asked me for a cigarette. He says he will give me one if I see him again, if I need a cigarette later. If he does, that is a sign. The genius is in writing it all down only. It does not matter what the words are, the genius thinks to write them down. One insect can bite one man many times, but the man will still live. Many small insects can kill a man. I am one insect. I cannot kill anything, but I can bite. All the people can kill God together if they bit him all at the same time.

Who wrote this he asks her. Who wrote this?

A woman in one city misses a man she spent a day with in another city.

Things I miss about him, how he made me feel like I was worth making love to, as he would say. I want to make love to you, he would say. I miss how I felt while waiting for him to come make love to me. Why did I want him to make love to me? Because I wanted to touch him and I wanted him to touch me, and I usually don't want that from people. I miss how he would quote me, nobody except him remembers what I say, even though he has only known me for a little while and we have been apart. I miss the way he said hello when he called. He says hello like children do, as if he is shocked people could hear each other over the phone. Every time, he said it the exact same way. Hello was the only word he said that never changed no matter what mood he was in. But what if some other man calls me and says hello that way? I don't want any other man to call me. I don't want them to touch me and I don't want to touch them. This thing would have to be done with somebody who you want to touch you. It will be all right though, as long as I look the same. I am sure I will meet somebody I want to touch me again in time. I don't want to look older. What will change about me at forty? I will go gray. But, I can dye my hair. I can get it conditioned too. It is not thick hair, but there may still be a lot of it left at forty. Maybe it is good my hair will thin out because there may be too much of it now. I will have to take care of my skin. The skin on my face used to be so much smoother. Now look at you. It will look even worse. What about the cellulite on my thighs? That will only get worse. Not unless you don't buy a car and walk to go where you need to go in this city. What about my stomach? That will get worse, your fat stomach. But I won't have kids, because nobody will make love to me, so maybe my stomach will be the same as the stomachs of other old women by then. But, I have to look better than I do now. Stop picking at the skin on your face. Yes, so it looks good. And don't have children. But if you have a child then maybe somebody has seen your body and made love to it before. My feet will probably look the same. My calves will look the same. Have you seen the calves of those rich old ladies who come in on Sundays? But that's only because they lose muscle tone and expose their calves to the sun. You will be walking everywhere with your legs covered. Your calves will be fine. What is the difference between a twenty-year-old foot and your feet? I am not sure. I have never compared my feet now with a twenty-year-old foot. Calves will be fine, I think. Thighs might be the same with some walking. No, with a lot of walking, with a lot of walking. Stomach will be worse, but might be the same if I don't have children. Arms and hands, I am not sure about. You should cover up your hands and arms too. The skin on the face is what I have to worry about most. The skin of my face.

The woman in the city misses a man in another city.

I will leave him a message. I will just say, hi, I miss you. You are the only person I have ever really, really wanted this much. I dream of tracing the outline of your face with my lips. I dream of it. I relive the day we spent together in your city over and over again. But we can be friends still if you want. I will tell him about how on the plane back from his city to my city I couldn't tell when there was turbulence because my stomach felt as if I were diving down through the clouds the whole time anyway. I will be fine. It will be fine. We will be friends. My face will be fine. My feet are all right. My hands are good. My neck and shoulders are all right too. Everything will be fine. I will look the same and will be able to be touched by somebody I want to touch me. My feet will be fine. I can always get pedicures too. My hands too, manicures, and keep them away from the sun. I will have gained weight, but I can walk everywhere and not eat as much as I do now. I will have to dye my hair. I will have to make sure the skin on my face looks fine. The skin on my face will have to look at least as good as it does now.

The woman in a city misses a man in another city.

What do you like about him anyway? The way he drives. I may never like the way a man drives ever again. I never even knew to like the way a man drives so much before. He was not scared to drive through such a big city. He wove his way in and out of people and cars and bicycles, as if it was only an instinct. I don't know how I kept from touching him while he drove. He said we could do that when he came to visit me. He would drive and I would touch him. There is just something about somebody who can walk, drive, eat and drink all over a city with you for fifteen hours. It was fifteen hours, he picked me up at around eleven in the morning and we got back to his bedroom at around three in the morning the next day. Or sixteen hours, maybe. Somebody who could talk to, be with, you from eleven in the morning until three in the morning the next day. The way he talks with that little accent. How honest he can be suddenly, so blunt. I guess that would be his spontaneous honesty. How well he knows his city. How cute he sounds at night when he is sleepy on the phone, like a baby. He said I was the type of girl who could motivate him to grow up. What does that mean? I don't know, but he said things like that, good things about me. This is real intimacy he once said. He leaves the best messages. That one he left after I sent him the picture of me alone in bed was my favorite. It said exactly this: love it, so hot, just came very hard, wish you could send me more, you are amazing and incredibly sexy, I love everything about you, can't wait to have those panties. He was so cute, when I sent him a message saying I will come to the city to see you, he wrote back who is this. Just to be funny, to make me jealous. Who is this? He knew it was me. When I said we should try to stop talking because we live in different cities he left me a message saying exactly this: you're killing me, I can't believe you won't call right now. I can't call because I swore on my car. You know how important my car is to me. He loves to drive around that city. And all those pictures alone in bed . . . bent over, legs crossed, standing in front of mirrors, partly covered with blankets. It is maybe a good thing he isn't here.

He would have to actually see me naked. He must have figured out all those pictures were taken with my back arched and my thighs together for a reason. At least you can't see texture in the pictures from a phone camera. All the cellulite, the stretch marks, the little ingrown hairs. It is better, he never came.

The woman in the city misses a man in another city.

Every time a man I want to touch me brings my face closer to his face with his hands to kiss me I start to shiver from my chest, down to my gut, then down. Not always while they are doing it, but when I think about what they did later. I remember their hands on my face and feel something like water trickling down the center of my body. He has to do it right though. Place one hand on my face and slowly inch my face towards his mouth with his hands. He did it right. That's all there is to it. And I wanted to kiss his shoulders. The minute he told me he had hair on them I placed hair on the shoulders I had been imagining kissing. Whatever he would have told me he was I would have imagined, and then imagined kissing. The minute he said he had back hair I placed hair on the back I had been imagining. It was a back with hair I held on to from beneath him, my arms wrapped around him. Later he said something about hair and acne scars and it became a hairy back with acne scars I imagined kissing, or washing, or massaging. Tell me how much of you there is and I will imagine it, and I will kiss it.

The woman in the city misses a man in another city.

I wanted him to scrub my back. There are all these marks on my back from the bedbug bites I got from living in that building. There are bites I wanted him to scrub off. I wanted to show him my scars from all the bedbug bites, and wait for him to kiss them. I wanted him to smell me and say something nice about how I smell. I feel sometimes that I am only a thing, or something, a spirit maybe, but in a bad way. I feel as if my body is dead and I am just this thing that keeps moving in it. My body is my own casket. I wanted him to make me feel my body again. He didn't know it, but I would move the phone away from my face and come to the sound of his voice sometimes. I would feel a sensation travel from my chest to my gut to my crotch when I saw his number on the screen. It felt like little water blossoms bursting in me. Stop. Stop. Just read, or something. Who is it? Who said every word was once a poem? Who said you take back words to arrive, you take back meaning to arrive at an essence? I wish I had kissed him that night. I relive that day and kiss him every time he says something. I wish he would come see me, so he could kiss my back in the mornings, and put his face in my neck. I will be fine. I will look fine when I am old. I will look at my own feet and like them. It is better to enjoy looking at your own feet than to wait for someone to want to look at them. It is better to like your feet since you have to look at them all the time, whether anyone else can see them or not. Either way it is better to have pretty feet.

A woman in the city misses a man in another city.

The problem is that every time I went anywhere in this city while I was waiting for him I thought of what it would be like to be there with him. I thought about whether he'd like this particular bar or that restaurant. I made memories that hadn't happened yet, that haven't happened. It's strange. I have to stop this. I can't keep thinking about what he would think of every place I go in this city. This Polish bar has really cheap high end vodkas and good cabbage. This bar used to be a church, and he would have appreciated the sacrilege. All right, how to make this stop. Think about more important things. I may owe the hospital a thousand dollars even though I already paid what I owed to the insurance company. I wouldn't have had done it if I knew it was going to cost this much money. It probably wouldn't have turned into cancer anyway. I paid twenty dollars every time I went in, and the deductible or deposit or whatever they called it, and eighty percent of the cost already. And that medicine for the infection cost me seventy five dollars. I should have never let them convince me to do it. If this thing with the insurance company gets cleared up, then I will feel better. At least I don't have to spend all that money I was going to spend at the salon if he had come. I was going to get the deep conditioning treatment, so when my hair gets in his face while we are lying next to each other it doesn't feel coarse. And my underarms needed waxing, so when he lifted my arms to pin them over my head he didn't see stubble. And my legs had to be shaved, and the bikini line waxed so if he was going to do anything to me for any reason there would be nothing there except that mole. I would have needed a pedicure so if my feet were rubbing up against him they would feel smooth. Maybe I would have gotten a facial too to get rid of blackheads and whiteheads. And a back facial to help with the scarring from the bedbug bites. Now I have saved all that money. I really wanted to spend all that money. I wanted to feel like I was beautiful for somebody for a day or two. All right, think about something else. The problem is I have been walking around imagining where we would go. So, every bar, every restaurant was just being inspected so I knew where to take him. Really good Italian food here, pride themselves on original Tuscan recipes. Bad Cuban food here, but really good Mojitos, very minty. Now everything in this city reminds me of him, even though he has not been here with me. He has never been here with me. I thought he might let me wash him. I have always wanted to wash somebody's body for them. Not shower with him, but wash him. I would have started from the top of his head, washed his hair carefully, and worked my way down to his toes. I really thought I would get to wash him. I just hate this feeling, that's all. It's just a feeling. It's not just anybody you will want to wash, or anybody that would just let you wash them. Now I don't want anybody to ever see me naked alone in bed again, because I know I am ugly now. I look at myself and I am uglier than I ever have been. It's the way I imagined he would say my name while he was inside me, because of all the things he would say about making love. He says my name like nobody else does. He doesn't pronounce it like my mother does, he doesn't pronounce it like my friends do. He says it in this other way. He says my name as if we are young. That is how I could imagine somebody would have said my name if I had friends when I was much younger. If I had friends at school, or even at a church or something then. This has to stop. I want to vomit a little, always, all the time. It is bearable, but uncomfortable. It's as if this feeling is saying here is where your chest is, here is where your stomach is, here is where your vagina is all day long. I can't keep feeling like this. Think about something else. Look at that homeless man over there. Think about all the homeless people in this city. Look at the homeless people. They are probably worried about more than who is and isn't going to come fuck them. He uses the words to make love though. Who will, or will not, come make love to them. I want to come make love to you. I shouldn't have to pay the hospital. I already paid the insurance. I already paid. That homeless man doesn't look worried about anything anyway. It probably has come close to five hundred dollars already. I paid every time I went in, and the deductible thing, and I needed that one hundred dollar tube of medicine for the infection afterwards. Look around it's a beautiful day in the city. The homeless people can't sit outdoors at a café and enjoy the day. He made me feel so beautiful. I feel so ugly now. It's all right because nobody will see my body ever again. All right, why do you feel ugly? I feel ugly because a man who saw me naked alone in bed made me feel beautiful but doesn't want to see me anymore. Well, you go see him then. I can't, he told me not to do that. This feeling will go away then. Feelings always go away. Like the feeling he felt for you when he made you feel beautiful, that went away. I can't ever trust this feeling again. Even when I'm old and somebody I want to touch me wants to touch me, I just won't trust it. You won't ever stay beautiful to anyone. You didn't stay beautiful.

THERE ARE LITTLE BUGS IN THE BIG CITY

She was the only one, the only one he wanted then. She was a beautiful brown haired girl, an actress. After she performed brilliantly in the school plays, she would party. He saw her from the window dancing once. She was dancing so hard, sweating so much, she had to take her shirt off. He wanted to be able to dance with her like the other actors, but he knew these types of things don't happen to him. He could go in that house and stand up next to her but he would still not be able to dance. He was closer to her watching her through a window.

The other one he imagines often. The one he could have loved so much he would have defended wholly. He imagined that if another man were to hurt her he would feel violated with her, for her, and would be willing to sacrifice his body for her if she wanted. She is the one he loved so much he could have fought for out of sacrifice, not pride. It is after he met her that he stopped understanding why any man would grab at a woman's body without being asked, why men do anything harsh at all to women. But he knew men did cruel things and he would rather have sacrificed his body to violence than her weaker body. He imagined she could love him so much that in their old age she would have wanted nothing more in life than to limp to him, a quiet sick old man. She would limp towards him to give him food, medicine, and kisses with her dried out lips. He imagined that she wanted to kiss him once for every word he could not say out loud, for things he never said. And even when they were old she would take him inside her with such agony in the extent of her pleasure he would feel he was large and young still. So large only a woman who loved him could stand to open up wide enough to have him in her.

This one he knew could have happened to him. The one he had to tell about the bedbugs could have happened to him, could have actually happened. After the drink she asked if she could sleep over. He was forced to admit there were insects that eat his blood living where they would rest. He was happy when he explained how painful it was for him to wake up in the middle of the night afraid and she didn't say anything about big men being scared of little bugs. He had sensed already she was capable of those kinds of jokes. Instead she walked out of the bar with him silently. And just as he thought everything inside him would be shaken up and he would start tearing up because he is alone always in a room with insects who take his blood she touched his arms. She kept walking with him just as he thought he would have to swallow shame like it is his own phlegm. She knew it wasn't his fault. He did everything he was supposed to do to kill them but he couldn't control what the people in the other apartments did. She is the one who for one moment that night while walking down that street he thought he could survive a life with. She is the one who could have survived a life with him. Until her naked body, so hot on the bed, in the middle of the night brought him even more discomfort than the thought of those little bugs. She will not get bit, he thought, she is nuclear. The anxiety he felt over the bugs who live with him on the bed was overwhelmed by the anxiety of her possibly living with him and sharing his bed. The lack of sleep will make him feel like little hands are tucking at his eyelids all day tomorrow. Where are the bugs? Why did she come here? At that moment he realized that all people are only ever good at one thing. Either they can dance well, or they can kiss you well, or they can teach you how to do something you don't know how to do but have always wanted to learn. They can pay no attention to what else lives on your bed with you and still want to sleep next to you. Where are the bugs? He remembers that there is one in the little plastic bag. He put it there when he found it this morning to show the landlord later. It could be suffocating, suffering. He could get up and kill it. It had just eaten. Its blood, the blood inside it, is his blood, and it will smear the bag. He could press on it lightly and his blood would smear a bag. It lives with his blood. They most often feed before the break of dawn. He knew that at least. One bug would come out soon to eat off of his body.

The bugs are babies with teeth and he is their mother. He decided that when it appeared he would let it walk on his finger. They can barely move. They move so slowly. They move like crippled old men these bugs. He would lift his finger and kiss it with his lips because it is all right by him if it crawls inside his mouth. He knew the bug would not realize it could live another day without his blood and so it would want him. It can live, but it can't grow and grow without him. He knew that like everyone, the bug does not feel like it has blood until it takes or gives it.

The woman in the city who misses a man in another city writes on the bus.

What will you have this summer without him? The same things I had before him. The grass will be the same. Bright green grass with little lavender flowers that you can see from the windows of the buses. Lavender flowers bursting in spurts on grass like sea foam, no like champagne bubbles, or like anemones in the sea or something beautiful. The sun is making its heavy, thick yellow outline around clouds. God lives in the sky. I will still be able to look at the bodies of men if I want to, but I will not kiss one of their bodies everywhere. I wanted to kiss him everywhere. I would have kissed every place of his body, anywhere. Now I will be able to stare at a man's body the way I can stare at a tree. I will have grass that moves like silky hair moves in wind, or hair that moves like grass. Dandelions have heads made of champagne bubbles. Sea foam, or floating feathers. Think about unhappy marriages. It is not good to love anyway, it is a feeling, it never lasts. There are women who had men who let them wash them, and kiss them everywhere, and now they feel sick all the time too. Better to not have had it at all. Better for things to be taken away early. Somebody will wash him, but it will not be you. Somebody he will want to wash him. Somebody he would leave his city for. How can somebody want somebody else for so long anyway? They want her long enough to get married to her. If he kissed me right now, his mouth would feel like flower petals. Flower petals? Like petals stroking my body, like smooth, clean, bright tongues on my chest. That's what I could have had this summer. If his hands had moved all the way up and down my body, palms open, to press me down to a bed I would have been all those dandelion seeds floating away. I sent him so many pictures of the sky with messages. In this one you can see God, I wrote once. It was supposed to be funny. I know he doesn't believe in God. I believed in God more when I thought of him, when I was waiting for him. The thick yellow light who presses against the clouds. There are all kinds of shades of blue in the sunlight this summer.

The woman in a city misses a man in another city.

If you just keep reading, you will be able to concentrate. You just have to say one thing about art. You can say you think all art is only a recreation of what is already found in nature. We recreate sounds to resemble an emotion to make music. We recreate images to make a bad feeling, an emotion, solid. All the smells, textures, and tastes in art are taken from nature. But they are really only a bad feeling, or a good feeling. There is the feeling of floating slightly above water, water blossoms bursting on my skin as I float slightly above water while staring at the sun. When the sun is so bright behind clouds that you know you wouldn't be able to see it if it weren't for those clouds, naturally, you assume it is God. Your body can't stand it, but you want it still, so it must be God. What would him making love to you have made you feel? Well, the feeling of dangling safely like branches in wind, the feeling of being able to lift slightly above the grass so that it brushes against the bottom of my feet, the feeling of floating slightly above water so that it blossoms and bursts and licks the skin of your back. The smooth lumps of water, the lips of the closed mouths of water brushing against you. The hope of seeing the sun, or those other sensations you imagined you can't stand, but could want. What would you being in his arms do for you? That feeling of being carried, that a child feels, that you couldn't remember feeling before you were in his arms. You are grown now, you can't be carried, your whole body can't be contained only on one person's chest. What would him cupping your face to bring it closer to his face to touch your lips with his lips do for you?

Even if you knew the earth was flat you would still wonder why the horizon curves slightly. The clouds could be women bending down to clean hard floors, or bushels of hay, or homeless men sleeping. But they most often look like the foam on waves on the ocean. In heaven as it is on earth, what is above is below.

The woman in the city misses a man in another city.

He knew to punish first. It is best to punish first and early. But maybe he feels the same way about me as I do about him. He just knew it wouldn't work out because nothing does, especially if two people live in different cities, and he just wanted to hurt me first, before I could hurt him. All the men I have wanted to touch me must have known this about the future. In the spring things are born. They live in the summer and they die in the winter. Maybe I only wanted to do things with him that could only be done in cities anyway. First we went to a restaurant, then we walked around the park, then we went for tea and dessert, then we went to see a show, then we went to a bar. We were going to walk in parks, eat in restaurants that have the best food of their kind of food, and he was going to drive around men delivering food from cheaper restaurants. I wanted to wash him because nobody can see every place of their own bodies like somebody else can. We leave it up to the water to go everywhere, but the water can't see you either.

The woman in the city misses a man in another city.

When I saw his number on the telephone screen I sank, a sensation would travel from my chest to my gut to my crotch. It felt as if water blossoms were bursting inside me. Now I want somebody to take off my body. My whole body is a hangnail on my mind. I can't really feel it unless I touch it. But I know it is there so I think I can feel it, and need to get rid of it, so I can feel something else. I want it to die. We went to a restaurant. We watched a movie there and then he made the waiter give me change even though they said they couldn't break the bill. Then we went to the park. We walked around and talked about all the other people and watched somebody filming a commercial. Then we went to a modern classical music show or something like that. He fell asleep and I put my head on his shoulder. Then we, no, we went to the park. Then we went to that teahouse. We went to the fancy teahouse where I got chocolate on my face and clothes. Then we went to a show. Then we went to that bar where we saw that woman kissing that man. When I thought of him coming to visit me my cells opened and tried to burst their way out of my skin and into the air. I have to reign them back in. Bring in the cells of my body. Tell my skin to be quiet again because nothing is going to happen. He is everywhere. I talked to him once and there was sunlight in this room. I felt what I felt during sunlight. Now he is in the sunlight. The sunlight reminds me of him. The sunlight reminds me I am alone. I will not have hands on me this summer.

All right.

All right, think.

Why do you feel sick?

Because I wanted him.

Why does that make you sick?

Because he doesn't want me.

Why do you care?

Because it means he doesn't want me.

But what does that mean about you?

He won't call me. He doesn't like me. He doesn't want me.

But what does it mean about you?

He doesn't want me like I want him.

He doesn't want you like you want him. Nobody you want will ever want you.

What do you feel? Sick, nauseated, tense, and tensile, jittery, all my organs are fluttering, shivering.

What would make you feel like that?

He isn't here. He doesn't want me.

Why does that make you feel sick?

I want him to want me.

But, why does it make you feel sick to not have what you want?

To not have who I want??

A woman in the city misses a man in another city.

You didn't know him, and you felt nothing was missing. Then I felt something for him now he is not something he is something missing. I miss a man wanting me, that's all. You just want a man. I need to go to a different city where the people are hungry, to remind yourself what's really important in life. I try to remind myself of the homeless, but I can't feel my body and they can feel theirs so really they are happier than I am. In a different city I will be able to feel my body, because there your body will be in more danger. I have to leave this city. One freckle on my forehead, that's fine. But two or three spots from scabs there too. My chin is spotted with scars from scabs. And now there are four new scabs on my chest from where I have picked at my skin. My chest has been so sensitive lately. It has been so hard to keep the skin from scabbing. Every time I rub on a patch or a bump of skin it turns red, then scabs, and then scars. The skin between my breasts is showing age, fine lines and huge pores there. There are stretch marks on my breasts and no children to show for it. What are these little spots all over your arms? My shoulders are fine though. My shoulders I accept. My hands are ok. And my feet are fine. I need to get my legs waxed and my arms waxed. And I have to do something about the scars on my back. My hair is going gray and my skin is discolored from twelve scars that were on my face. I have to whiten my teeth, teeth get discolored with age. There are stretch marks on breasts. My neck is fine. My neck I accept.

People in the city.

She can't kill it if she doesn't have the money. She has to find the money. She can't find the money. She can't keep it because she doesn't have the money. It can't keep growing inside her because she can't feed it once it comes out of her. But if she doesn't have the money to kill it then it will grow. If it keeps growing it will have to come out of her body and then she will have to feed it but she doesn't have the money. She could kill it herself while it is still inside her but how without dying herself? She can ask somebody to kill it for her but why would they do it without her giving them money? If it keeps growing and it comes out of her then she will have to feed it but she can't. She can let it die after it comes out of her because then she will have killed it. Maybe it will die by itself inside her. Maybe it will die when it comes out of her because it will starve on its own without her having to kill it.

PEOPLE KILL PEOPLE IN THE CITY

She really wants to stop panicking. Nobody is going to kill her tonight. The doors are locked, the windows are locked. Nobody is coming for her. He is not coming for her. The man screaming, how do you think it makes me feel don't you ever think about how it makes me feel, does not live with her. He lives in the next apartment. She can't stop feeling this panic. She sees shadows where they shouldn't be, in lit places where shadows can't be. She sees marks on the walls that she thinks are shadows. There is no logic to this. It's psychological. There is something psychologically wrong with her. She is so worried about herself that she begins to cry. She is terrified of somebody, a man, appearing out of nowhere with a knife and she is crying because she might be going crazy. She is crying because she thinks she is going insane.

She is scared because she thinks somebody is coming to kill her tonight. She knows all the other people in this city are not scared when their doors and windows are locked and there is nobody in their lit apartments. She wants to believe she is normal. She wants to remember things other women have told her about times they were frightened in their locked apartments for no reason at all. It's just like that feeling people have when they are outdoors and they're worried about being bit by ants or mosquitoes or other insects. They begin to feel them crawling on their bodies even when they are not there. She can feel the sensation of them crawling all over her, but when she looks at her skin there is nothing there. She can't see anybody in the apartment right now, but everywhere she looks there are weapons he can use to kill her when he comes. These cords he will use to strangle her. These pillows he will use to suffocate her. And everything in the kitchen he will use to take apart her body. All the metal objects he will use to gouge the inside of her body are in the kitchen. She feels she knows this will happen tonight even though there is no reason for it to happen tonight, or any night. But she knows there is a reason, because it happens, because it has happened to other people whose windows and doors were locked, because it is something that happens to people and has already happened to other people. She doesn't want to become crazy. She doesn't want it to get to that point, because that point is always there inside her, because other women have died this way, because that happens too. She might have to live on the streets if she goes crazy. She will be crazy and homeless if she can't control herself. She doesn't know how to stop this. The only other time she wants to stop herself from feeling something and can't is when she is in love with a man who she knows doesn't want her but she still can't help wanting him anyway. It feels exactly the same way, because she can't stop, but better maybe because she isn't terrified, she is hopeful. She never thought anything could feel worse than that feeling of being in love with a man who doesn't want her and not being able to stop waiting for him to call or walk by or say or do something he will never do. If none of those other men she has waited for before could stop themselves from disappointing her, then why would the one she is waiting for now, to come and kill her, not disappoint her? Now that she knows how bad this feels though she wishes she could be waiting for a phone call from a man she wants to call who won't call instead, at least then she isn't shaking. It's the same feeling in a way because she can't control her thoughts and she is waiting for something to happen that won't happen, but it is a better feeling because it is hope not terror, at least until she really realizes . . . It's just that when she is in love with a man she expects to see him everywhere she goes and is disappointed when he is not suddenly walking down the same hall or crossing the street. She looks up now and expects to see the man with a knife in the doorway. The same irrational expectations, but she now realizes that wanting somebody to call when nobody will call her feels a little better than waiting for somebody to come kill her. But if no man ever has called while she waited then no man will ever kill her while she waits. She must know that she will not die tonight. Every time she has had her cards or her palm read the reader has told her she will have a long life. She wonders if maybe simply pretending she doesn't care if she gets killed tonight might help. If she thinks of her slashed body and sees white blood instead of red . . . If she imagines a knife plunged in her exiting her body a dark shade of blue instead of a dark shade of red . . . Why is she so scared of being murdered? What would it feel like anyway? Probably just like . . . nothing, but she can't stop shaking. Even though if a man pushed her down and cut her throat open, it would probably be painless. What will she feel right afterwards, those few seconds, while she knows she is dying? Probably . . . nothing. Why would any of this make her heart beat out of her chest then? What if she imagined her body cut open and all her blood was bright yellow, not red? What if she imagined a whole field of women with slit throats hung upside down on spikes, naked, with forest green blood dripping slowly from their necks onto their faces. Earth brown blood flying everywhere as somebody's head flies off their body is not terrifying. Nobody gets told they will be murdered when they have their cards or palms read. Why would anybody have let her know that? Anything can happen at any moment. This has happened before to other people in this city. The only thing that could calm her down right now is if nobody had ever been murdered in their own apartments in this city. The only thing that should comfort her right now is that not once has a man she was waiting to love her actually loved her even though other people have been loved by men they wanted to love. Purple blood doesn't make anything better. Black blood makes everything worse, black blood is worse than red blood. Orange blood. Orange blood gushing out of her chest when he stabs her, that would be fine.

HUSHED

She opens her eyes and sees the sky. Today is a perfect day. The window is right next to her bed and she keeps her curtains open, so she can always see the skyline in the morning. Today has a perfect sky. It is a very blue sky and very clear. She doesn't have anything to do today either. Everything is fine at work. Everything is fine. Her mother is fine, not sick again, so she doesn't have to worry about her. She has friends, and her feelings haven't been hurt by a friend in a while. She has a good job and a nice apartment in a great city. And she had a date yesterday. She had a date with a perfect man. He is not too much younger, or older, than she is. He is good looking, educated, and charming. He cooked for her too. And he was charming. She can still feel where he was on her bed.

She gets up to go to the bathroom. She looks in the mirror and wonders if she looked that messy last night. Maybe it was good to look that messy though, unnoticeable at least. She has to do something about her hair. Her hair is too straight to really do anything creative with. Her hair is just too straight.

Today she wonders, for the first time in her life, what animal, if any, she most resembles. Not a pig really, but a warthog, maybe. Maybe she looks like a warthog. When she smiles, the way her cheeks curl, it can possibly look like she has tusks. She smiles and frowns repeatedly in the mirror. Her nose can be very pig like too, the way her nostrils are so obvious. And sometimes she thinks she has no mouth. No, she does not have a very prominent mouth. Yes, she kind of looks like a warthog. Even her forehead now is obviously the forehead of a warthog. How could she not have noticed this before today? She has a big warthog's head on a frumpy boy's body. This must be why she hates dancing in public. One of her friends always makes her dance when they go out. It starts with a simple come dance with me.

You go dance and I'll watch.

Fine, I don't want to dance alone. We'll just sit here.

No, you go dance. Honestly, I just don't feel like it.

Come on. Come dance with me. Do it for me, please.

All right, I will later. Let me drink first.

You can drink while we are dancing.

I'll just finish my drink first.

She ends up on the dance floor eventually, feeling all eyes on her. Her uncomfortable body, and its uncomfortable movements, are judged by all the men watching her. Men who are thinking about women and how they move their bodies. This is a dumb way to move an ugly body. Suddenly she realizes that all those men who have ever watched her dance must have been thinking exactly that. She does not ever want to dance but she does it, she dances sometimes. It makes her feel dumpy.

In the future she will do something with her hair. But first she has to brush her teeth. The brush seems especially rough against her gums today. It seems as if the brush will move her gums up further and further until there is a small ridged space between her teeth and gums where blood will slowly dribble down. She can feel her gums get tighter and tighter as they are being taken in by the brush. The brush has a job to do and it is to take away the gums, take off all the gums, move them back, whether they want to go or not. Maybe she will stop brushing her teeth for a while, a couple of days or so. That way her gums get a rest. Unless, of course, he calls tomorrow and wants to see her again tomorrow, or in a couple of days. Maybe it would be good if he doesn't call her for a couple of days. Yes, that might be good so that she doesn't have to brush her teeth and her gums get a rest.

Maybe she should shower too. She usually showers before she goes to bed though. Maybe she should put on some clothes, go out and do something. Maybe she should even put some perfume on today. She never really wears any perfume, but she always has one bottle somewhere. She doesn't like how everybody can tell she has perfume on when she puts on perfume. She obviously does not smell that good naturally, nobody does. She also never knows if she put on too much. Years ago her college roommate would spray perfume on her even when she had said she didn't want any. Her roommate wouldn't even ask if she wanted to put any on, she would just spray it on her. It would sometimes get in her eyes and mouth because she was unprepared for it. And for the rest of the night she would have to smell like whatever her roommate sprayed on her. She knew that as finicky as her roommate was about her perfume if she had sprayed her with something that she liked the smell of, her roommate would have been furious. What could she have done though? Some conversations don't seem worth having.

Why did you just do that?

Do what?

Spray that stuff on me without asking?

I'm sorry. We're going out though, I thought you might want to smell good.

But you didn't even ask me first.

I love this perfume.

But you didn't ask me.

I'm sorry. I didn't think it would be such a big deal.

Don't spray perfume on me again.

Fine. What's wrong with you tonight anyway?

Then maybe her roommate would feel bad about having sprayed perfume on her. Maybe her roommate would feel dumb. She wanted to avoid all that. It is better to just allow people to be themselves around you, without making them feel dumb. So she would just walk out with the perfume on and explain to herself why it might be a good thing to have perfume on. It made her sick sometimes, all that perfume would get in her eyes.

Shower. Don't shower. Shower. Don't shower, don't shower. She resists the urge to try and scrape at her skin because she feels there is no reason to indulge that urge. Something is wrong with her head today. It is making her sick.

She needs some music. The stereo is across from her bed, also by the huge window. With only her underwear on, she bends her body so she can fiddle with the dials. This she does most mornings so she can listen to music while she is getting ready to go to work. Today, however, she becomes more and more anxious as she imagines her body as a target. She imagines somebody watching her from one of the other apartment buildings. He is chuckling and snickering, planning to shoot an arrow at her. He will shoot an arrow into her anus because she is bent over, she is a target. If she does not move away quickly she will be in a great deal of pain. The arrow may go up and out through her mouth if she does not move away.

She turns off the radio and goes back to bed. She was so proud of her bed yesterday. All the shades of blue on one bed made such a beautiful bed. The fact that she chose so many shades of blue and put them all on one bed is one of the signs that she has a good life, a life of her own making. He must have noticed that.

Maybe she doesn't feel well just because of the wine. She usually doesn't have that much wine, but she got caught up in the moment yesterday. How many glasses of wine were there? One before he came over, because she was happy and nervous at the same time. One on the couch with him, one at the kitchen table, one on the couch again, with him. A total of four glasses of wine, but they may have been very full glasses. Maybe it was really more like five, or six, glasses of wine. She shouldn't be drinking that much. She can't be sure what is going on with her because she drank so much. Maybe she is too old now to be drinking that much and that's what's making her sick. She can smell him still on the bed and that doesn't seem good for her stomach. Something is not right today. But it is a perfect day. Everything is right in her life. Work is fine, and she has friends, and she even has a boyfriend now, maybe.

If he calls, and she is happy to hear his voice, then nothing is wrong. If he calls and she does not feel sick when she hears his voice then there is really nothing wrong. It is no big deal to her. She is probably just nervous because he may not call again. Yes, if she knew whether or not he would, or wouldn't, call she wouldn't be so queasy. Maybe she should wash the sheets because her stomach is off today. Then she can stay in bed all day and think about him.

She recaps in her mind. She starts from the very beginning so as to anticipate the moment he walked in the door yesterday. He is very good looking.

She met him through Margaret at work. Margaret told her that they would be perfect together because he is so mature and so ready to settle down. He has been one of Margaret's best friends for a long time. He and Margaret tried to date and see if anything was there, but fortunately for her, there wasn't. Margaret told her about the time they tried to have sex. Years ago they went back to her place drunk and slept on the same bed. He darted his tongue in and out of Margaret's mouth, which turned Margaret off. He kept trying to rub on Margaret's hips with his groin and she could feel him limp against her. Margaret was so turned off at that point that she had to turn around and pretend to be sleeping. He stopped rubbing up against her then. This story made him seem impotent and feckless. But Margaret insisted that he was very mature and very kind. There was just no chemistry between them she told her. She also told her about the times he had been there for her without wanting anything in return. He is just one of those people, a good friend, a rare catch. So Margaret took her along for a drink. She and her friend had already planned to meet up. She could meet him and see what she thought. He was surprisingly good looking for somebody who would rub his dead groin on his friend's hip fecklessly. His voice was very deep and his movements were very slow. She liked him. He looked at her intently when she spoke. But he didn't call right away. He waited a week, which was good because it made her very excited to hear from him when he did call. He decided they should meet at a fast food restaurant. He ordered a coke, that he paid for, and she had a hamburger, that she paid for. The conversation was good though. He could talk about anything. She knew she really liked him when they were talking about why people have children. She thought it important to bring up all kinds of philosophies and theories on why childrearing is, and is not, a selfish act. He said it was all very simple.

Children just make some people happier.

Not all people. You are making a human life you know? The implications of . . .

Children make people happier because they make their day to day lives about something other than theoretical implications.

He spoke slowly, moved slowly, and always seemed sure of what he thought. He could talk about his work, but without complaining, or seeming too enthusiastic. He could talk about travel, and the cultures of different countries he'd been, but without being judgmental, or naive. He knows all kinds of things. He is a man of the world.

They talked on the phone a few times after that. Mostly to work something out so they could see each other again. He turned out to be very mature. He called when he said he would call. He called at the exact time he said he would call.

Yesterday was their second date. He came over to cook for her. This made up for the hamburger. It made him perfect. It was very reasonable to not spend money on somebody you don't know yet. It's not like he's desperate. But when they got to know each other better he cooked for her, an intimate giving gesture. He is thrifty and loving. She was so nervous that she had to have just one drink before he came over. No one has ever cooked for her before. Usually she has a couple of dates with a bad looking person, somewhere mediocre, and she never gets called again, and doesn't really want to get a call most of the time. Here was a real man coming to make pasta for her. They talked about ingredients and wine like a team. He made her feel as if she was part of a team. He walked in and he looked good. He is good looking. He brought his own spices for the sauce, but no flowers. That was good though because flowers are a waste of money, and he is too sincere for superficial gestures. He is not interested in superficial gestures and the spices are necessary so he can cook for her. They drank wine. He cooked. He looked especially good cooking because he was moving very slowly and he was making the kitchen warm and nice smelling. They could talk about everything and laugh a little, not in that silly way though, in a very mature way. They laughed the way people do when they are having a mature, adult conversation. He made her feel as if she can be herself, but not get away with anything. He lets her know when he thinks she is not thinking logically, but he lets her express herself patiently.

If they had money then they wouldn't be saying that . . .

That is not necessarily true. Lots of people who have that much money know what to do with it, and what it is really worth to them.

It must be hard to work for something like . . .

If you are only doing it for the money, maybe.

They sat on the couch after dinner and he got close to her, facing her. He looked into her eyes as she spoke, he smiled perfectly. It was not too big a smile, one that would be on the verge of immature, but not a smirk either.

I think it is easier to travel alone if you're a man.

In certain ways, maybe, but not in every way.

I have a friend who has a geography degree and she said it hasn't been difficult at all to find jobs in this area.

Isn't it always less difficult to find jobs in some areas than in others depending on what you do?

I'm sorry about the books on the floor. I always think I will get to them but I don't.

Why don't you?

You know, I just get busy.

Doing what?

By the time I come home from work, relax for a while, eat, take a shower, it's time to go to bed and do it all over again the next day.

It's all about momentum. It would only take an hour out of your day to pick something up and read it.

Then he reached for her face and kissed her. So he does dart his tongue back and forth in people's mouths, but she thought it was cute. Kissing him felt really good actually because it meant that he really had come over to cook for her, and that the pasta meant what she thought it meant. Then everything he did to her felt better and better as he kept doing things to her. He made wonderful noises too. He was not enthusiastic enough to be gauche, but not quiet enough to not be enthusiastic. He got up and slowly moved into the bedroom silently. She followed him. Despite the wine she was still so nervous that her heart wanted to beat right out of her chest. Here was a good looking man who wanted to cook for her and have sex with her. Everything was perfect. Then suddenly she wondered whether or not they should be doing what they were doing at all. Besides the phone calls, last night was only their second or third time in the same room with each other. But it was all so wonderful, him standing over a stove in the kitchen while she watched him move as she sat on the couch. She thought it would be a good idea to see how he felt about what they were doing. She should just bring it up, ask him quickly. He had only been inside her for about a minute when she asked him to stop. She whispered, Wait, stop. She thought he would stop and she would explain that she thinks maybe this isn't the right thing to do. That's when he would kiss her and talk her out of it. It's right because you are wonderful, and this has been wonderful, he would say. It's right because I have never felt so much for someone so quickly. She would stop him and say something pithy, or witty, about whether or not people should be doing what they were doing so soon after meeting each other. Stop, she whispered. Wait, stop. Stop. Stop. Stop. Stop. Stop. But he still kept going. Then his wonderful noises started to sound like loud grunts. He couldn't hear her, maybe. Maybe he just couldn't hear her. Stop, she had whispered. He still kept grunting. Was she there? He didn't know she was there. Stop it. What to do? What to do? She could scream.

Stop it! Stop it! Stop! Just stop!

What, what are you screaming for?

I wanted you to stop and you didn't . . .

Sorry, I was just trying to make love to you.

Are you deaf or something?

Actually I am. I lost my hearing in the same car accident that took my little brother two years ago.

Sorry about that.

I have to go.

I'm sorry. I didn't mean anything by it. It's just that I had been asking you to stop and you didn't listen so I thought I should scream so you can hear me.

I have to go. I feel stupid for coming over in the first place.

Instead of having that conversation she decided she could just stop asking him to stop and lie there. He would stop eventually and she could stare at him in the meantime. No. No. No. No, stare at the walls. This is taking a while she thought. One. Two. Three seconds. The walls, she realized then, have billions of little faceless, fast crawling, mindless, colorless insects darting all over them. Maybe every surface does if you really take the time out to stare at it, really look. She wished they had turned the lights on. She always gets a little frightened when she is alone in the dark.

He stopped when he was all finished eventually, and rolled off of her. Everything was fine though. He wasn't rude or anything afterwards. He even rubbed her back while he was sitting up to get ready to leave. When she told him that he could stay if he wanted to, he turned around maturely smiling.

I think I better take off so I can wake up early tomorrow, the drive from your place with the traffic . . .

He kissed her goodbye. So, everything was fine. He didn't think there was anything wrong, obviously. What to feel about this? After all, not being heard is something she is somewhat used to. She always has to shorten her stories because everybody acts like she tells really long stories, but she doesn't think she does. They begin looking away mid-sentence, or they finish her sentences for her. All her friends do this to her.

He's the one that I told you . . .

The one that was married to Sandra, I know.

But I didn't even want to go because . . .

Because you thought Andrew would be there, I know.

One of her friends even thinks that she talks too loud and hushes her. She just tells her to hush while she is speaking. She will be talking while they are having lunch at a restaurant, or coffee at a coffee shop, and her friend will hush her. So she can't even finish her sentences at all when she is out with this particular friend.

This is only the feeling of not being heard. Last night may be making her sick only because of what her friends have done to her in the past. It must be residual discomfort and embarrassment from having been hushed so many times before. It has nothing to do with him. She shouldn't take it out on him. After all she has actually been told before to just get off of a chair she is sitting on because one of her friends wanted to sit there. He didn't do anything like that. He was never rude to her.

Can I sit in front I need the space for my crutches?

But if you sit in back then you can lay them on the back seat.

Can I just sit in front?

Can I sit by the light I'm reading?

But I'm reading too.

Well, do you need all that light?

And why shouldn't this man want to be with a woman who wants him so much, all the time, that when he is inside her she would never want to ask him to stop? Why wouldn't he want to be around somebody who could react to him not stopping by being flattered? Everybody wants that man. Nobody wants to feel stupid. Everybody wants someone who will react the way they want them to react when they do certain things. That is what makes her feel loved, it is probably what makes everybody else feel loved too. When somebody reacts to something she does in the way she wants them to react to it she feels as if she was not stupid for doing it. And she is tired of waiting for people's reactions to be what she needs them to be to feel loved. She seems to always be waiting for people to touch her when she's sad, or call her when they're angry. It is just silly. It is not mature. She can't live her whole life feeling like this.

She rolls around in her bed and smells him. She imagines him hushing her, like a mother hushes while trying to put her baby to sleep in her arms. He is hushing her as she asks him to stop. Stop. His hands move slowly towards her to gently cup her face. He looks right into her eyes, kisses her mouth gently over and over again. Then he brushes her cheeks faintly with his lips as he moves his lips closer and closer to her ears so he can whisper, hush. Hush, he whispers, as he kisses her ears slowly. He moves so slowly. She looks at him and whispers, stop, breathlessly. Her mouth is barely touching his mouth as she speaks, her eyes begging for him. Stop it. Stop.

Stop.

Hush. Just hush.

PEOPLE KILL PEOPLE IN THE CITY

You have to admit there's a stench to you.

It's in your head. It's all in your head.

It's not genetic but the things you learn at home make the difference, they make you smell.

We all wake up and need to go relieve ourselves.

We all think food tastes good and we kiss our children's faces.

Most of us, not all of us.

Sorry, I didn't mean to bring that up.

We all feel hurt when we walk towards somebody that we thought was waving at us that turns out to have been waving at somebody else.

We all need to eat. We are all happy when we eat.

If we are hungry, remember.

Everybody thinks warts are ugly.

That's not true.

Most people are sad when their children die. And we listen to music. We all make music somehow. Every group of people has hated and killed another one. We all murder.

But it's the way you do all those things that makes you disgusting.

But everybody makes strange sounds when they fuck and strange faces.

You laugh differently.

Everywhere men find something to do with other men and women find something to do with other women. Everywhere there have been prisoners and slaves who have tried not to cry as their master got off on their faces, but neither could help it. They pull their clothes up or down as they walk away and unintentionally cry. We all touch the part of our body that hurts. If it's the head we put our hands on our heads. We wonder why the people we thought should love us because they felt like they loved us, that is just how they felt to us, why they turned out to not want us. People eat together everywhere. And talk to each other

But the way you slurp when you eat is disgusting.

We all tell stories about what happened to us. We scream daddy or mommy in different languages when we are scared if we are young whether we are loved by daddy or not. Just because people do bad things doesn't mean they are bad.

It got to the point where it was pointless. You say that but what are you trying to say?

Or when you said I don't know anything.

Even if it's not true.

You have to say things to remember them the way you want to remember them. So there is a something made of them.

It's disgusting though. Your nails with the chipped nail polish that you won't take off. Don't you know how to look good?

When they say my name, it shrinks what is inside my body. What is contained within them, bodies. All they were then was just a body because you killed everything else inside them when you said that, made it so small it didn't exist. All they are is bodies so they have to use their bodies to get the stuff inside their bodies back. All they had before are hands to hold bombs with so that's what they do. If you take away their pride they will use their bodies if you threaten to take away their bodies they will give you their pride.

Do you remember? Your mother would wear nail polish sometimes and it would chip and she would just put more nail polish on the chipped polish and you could see that that's what happened by looking at her nails. It was ugly. You were disgusted by your mother.

If she had died right in front of me though I wouldn't dare want to wipe it off. I would miss it.

The shame becomes pride.

Then anger at all of those people who think it is disgusting to wear chipped nail polish.

Everybody has a different way of going about it.

Either by being really funny or really smart or eating a lot. Or trying to look really good or being very quiet.

I choose to be quiet.

Or being very talkative or being very friendly. Or being very forgiving. Or forgetful.

When something makes me sad I don't laugh. I eat alone.

The people that choose to be funny they have to laugh at everything.

Remember? Your mother came out of the bathroom smelling of wet dog. Then she walked around the table full of food and put food on her plate like this and it embarrassed you in front of all those people. She started laughing really hard and she has a strange laugh so everybody stared at her funny and you were so embarrassed.

Now I wish I had held her like I am holding you.

You would go back and hold her in front of everybody if you could.

All those other people around the table don't matter now.

And the time she laughed so hard she made those snorting sounds. And everybody looked at her funny, then just looked at her.

I wish I had held her.

She is not dead.

But there's no way to go back and make things better now I can only apologize but she won't listen to me because she is alive, she can't really hear me like you can.

Like I can.

I apologize and she says she doesn't remember.

Do you remember the man?

If that man who asked me not to pinch his nose because it hurt him, when I was just trying to be nice and funny, if he was one of you I would hate you even more.

You would really have reason to.

And that man who said that's a strange thing to get excited about when I was only trying to be nice.

He is one of us.

He degraded me by saying that.

That man made you wish somebody would say "oh, a little pain never hurt anybody." "Especially coming from you. A little pain never hurt anybody, but if you're causing it then I like it."

Your skin is so soft. I can kiss it.

It's cold now.

It's still softer than it was. I can kiss it if I want to.

You like cold skin better than warm skin. Is that why?

No, that's just the only way the skin keeps.

I'm cold.

You wouldn't have known how good this can be. You couldn't have known. I had to convince you just to bring you here, remember?

I thought you would do what you did, at first I didn't want it.

But now . . .

The only thing that makes me happy is to eat. That is the only thing that doesn't feel good only to make me feel bad later.

To eat.

To eat alone.

I wanted a teacher to be my friend. I left books in his class on purpose every day so I could go back and get them. I did it once and it felt good because we talked and laughed while I was in the classroom to get my book. So I did it again. And I did it again. It was hard to do the first time, because I thought he would know, I would be caught, but then I did it again and again.

He later told you to just grow up.

I'm sorry.

I'm sorry.

He told me to grow up. He wasn't my friend. He didn't think I was funny.

I grew up in this house. Everybody was so close you could hear what people were doing in the bathroom. You knew them like that. I was close to their bodies.

I know all people are as bad as I am.

It's just that I had never been spoken to for hours or laughed with before.

Then he went away, right?

He even found the notes me and God thought he would find if he was the one that was going to stay with us.

People don't stay unless they need you. That's why I can't be happy when I think about how everything good that somebody does to make me happy is only there so I can really feel the thing they will do to make me hurt later.

We all speak just to be talking, eventually.

People are really not good unless you know them like this.

Unless you know only their bodies.

Unless you like them in this way that I like you. That's the only time they are nice.

When I want to forgive a person I imagine that person dead too. I know it wouldn't matter how much they had hurt me if I could miss them. When I want to forget what they did to me I imagine myself dead like this. When I want to forgive myself I imagine myself dead like this. Thank you.

The only thing that felt good to me for a long time was to eat.

Bad things still happen even when you wait for the good things to happen and remind yourself the bad things are temporary. But it doesn't matter because, so are the good things.

The good things only happen so the bad things can be recognized immediately.

Felt instantly.

I would say to myself I am not really feeling this because I have felt this before and it went away, so I will just not feel this now, since I know it's not really how I'm feeling since it will change eventually.

Then even the golden rule fails you.

You try to be sensitive to others but you know that you can be cruel even when you are being kind. You don't want to talk to them about what happened to them because you think they don't want to remember it, like you wouldn't want to remember it, and they think you don't care about them because you don't want to talk.

I know. I started crying once and the man on top of me held my face in his hands and said it's ok. It's ok. I said "no, it is not ok." I just want to be normal right now. Don't you see that I want to be normal my first time being naked in bed with a man. But he thought he was being nice.

Right now it's just you and me.

Your body and me.

You and my body.

And nothing can make this bad.

Nothing will happen later to make us bad to each other. We have this and it will stay like this because we can't say anything to each other when we talk.

You can't take back what you say and people take what you say to mean things. It is what you mean really but if you rephrase it then they feel better about it. You say this is what I really meant and it really is just you rephrasing what they said they thought you meant when what they thought you meant already hurt you.

But when you rephrased it they thought you were better, so this made you feel like you really did mean something other than what they understood the first time.

The first time is the hardest. It's like seeing a red fire alarm then deciding to push it. Then pushing it, just to see what happens. Because you were thinking about pushing it and knew you shouldn't but wanted to see what would happen. Then the other times it's better though because it lasts longer, but nothing is like the first time.

The first time you do it you realize you can do anything now but you only want to do this thing again. It's that good, you only want to do it again. The first time you know people are like food. You can put them inside you. You can take what you need for your body from their body and your body lets go of the rest. Takes the good and lets go of the bad. That way love is not something good that feels bad later. Not something that will feel good only to show you how bad it can feel without it later. But what about when you are hungry. Food lets you know you are hungry because sometimes you don't have it. Because it isn't always there. I have to eat.

ON THE WAY TO WORK

The theme of this hotel must be French things. There is a bakery where you can buy what must be the best éclair in the city, that's proof. There is also this buffet style restaurant where you can order crepes. They have painted the sky indoors, so you feel like you are outdoors all the time. So the theme could also possibly be morning time. They painted the ceiling baby blue and white, for sky and clouds. With those lights strategically placed in the corners beating on the blue ceiling it feels more like the outside than inside any other building you have ever been in. This makes you sad, because you think that taking into account all that has happened to the planet already someday people really won't be able to go outside anymore. But it makes you happy because it means that when push comes to shove people will be able to recreate sky from memory. Paint and some lights, that's all it will take. When we can't breathe the air anymore because of the energy and waste that is used up and made by this city we will still have some kind of sky to look up to. Logically though, it isn't this city that's going to kill the sky. You don't know why you think it is. People have been thrashing after the sky with a blood thirst for a while now. They are happy to name the buildings skyscrapers which means they want them to scrape the sky. But you still can't help wondering how much the world could be spared if this city was turned off for just an hour a day, every day. But even if people eventually ended up having to turn cities off for a while, every once in a while, out of necessity it wouldn't be this city that gets shut off. It would be a city where many women walk home alone at night after working all day. You must not really care though. You care more about your cup of coffee and this éclair every morning than you do about the fate of the whole world. You are of this city now. You think it's all going to be all right though. You are thinking now that it's all right to live here. You are making a story. It's all right that this city exists. You think that you should not be panicked. You are not thinking about millions of children being split open by men in the alleys of these streets. You think this place doesn't remind you every day that children are being made to perform acts on and for men. You are not panicked. This city does not make you think about how human nature, being what it is, will only make for more and more rape and torture and slaughter of children in the future. Kill all the fat ugly people. That's who would go first, in this city. No matter what group of people you belong to in this city, people do not like the fat ugly people. Nobody in this city seems to like the fat ugly people. That's why it is so acceptable to degrade them publicly. They are even made fun of in movies and on television. It's funny for everybody when the woman who shows up on the blind date turns out to be fat. Such bad luck for the man, for any man, everybody laughs. Surely he could never love her. No man can. She's fat. He can only be nice to her maybe, out of the goodness of his heart because he is such a nice man. Remember that show with the fat man who lived across the way from the good looking, thin people. They poked him once with a homemade stick all the way from their apartment. They wanted to know if the ugly man was still alive. He had only been sleeping. They knew this because he moved. It moved. They all ran away from the window. Everybody could laugh at that. You can't laugh at poking black people to make sure they're alive anymore though. People in this city do not think that's funny, many of them are black. But fat people may always be funny, there are less of them here. If they wanted to be normal they would just lose weight. How could they have known that he was only sleeping? The sleeping bodies of thin people look asleep, at rest, at peace. The bodies of fat people always look dead, or they should be. But forget about that. I know, you can play the hoochie or ho game all by yourself. Ok, you look at one of these girls and you guess, just hoochie, or professional ho. Hoochie. Hoochies going home. That one too, hoochie. All right. There, there, ho. Yeah, I think you're right. You analyze why. She is dressed like just a hoochie, but she is wobbling in front of that car and trying to make eye contact with men who pass by. A man that seems to know her comes up to her, presses himself against her, and says something angrily. She throws her bag to the ground and walks off. He laughs at her. She remembers that she needs her bag and wobbles back for it. Even the hos can laugh at the fat people though. Remember that movie you saw a long time ago filmed in this city. There is a scene where a man grabs the prostitute by her ass to kick her out of the casino. You're not sure if it was right after she got raped by teenagers, or before. You imagine a man grabbing this prostitute by her breasts to kick her out of a casino. This makes you sad because you have breasts too. There is nothing about this that makes you happy. This thought makes you want to wear a metal bra. It makes you wish you had metal breasts, or a whole body made of pure steel. Why couldn't he just kick her out? Why wasn't that enough? Why did he put his hands on her ass? You comfort yourself with the thought that this hasn't really happened. But in this city you know it already has. Everything you could imagine could happen has already happened here. Hoochies. Hoochies walking into a bar. Hoochies going to a bar in the morning. Maybe they are meeting somebody, maybe they never went to sleep. You analyze the Hoochies' motivations behind wearing so little. They just want to have fun in the city. This sometimes means being drunk and possibly meeting some man. But who could you meet here for Christ's sake? You have been a hoochie. When you were a hoochie you kept your jacket on in bars though. Even in the summer when you did not have a jacket on you had a lot on. You didn't think you would have to wear so little to let men know you were a hoochie, you were new to the city. You thought they would just be able to feel the vibe and come up to you. You were wrong. You were a failure. It's all right that you were a hoochie though. You want to believe this, so you think that you know that every mistake you make will somehow lead you closer to true love, closer and closer to a man really falling in love with you. But what if it doesn't? Having nobody to have sex with in this city, where sex is the most effective way to sell things, would be alienating. In general, romantic love is one of the best ways for all people to keep themselves company, give themselves worth, but this city makes you feel that it is almost crucial. It has become something you wait for, the beginning and end of everything, like a happy afterlife perhaps. So it is all right that you used to go to these bars and get drunk and hope that somebody you could stand would start speaking to you. It is all right because someday somebody will love you for just that reason. This city is just another whore after all and look at how beautiful and strong it can be sometimes. Why can't men ever really, really be called whores? Must be for the same reason you can't as easily degrade them by grabbing their asses or chests. It could be related to how men see themselves as better looking than they actually are. Remember that study they did where they had men and women draw themselves. The women tended to draw women who were fatter, uglier by societal standards than they actually were. The men tended to draw men who were more attractive by societal standards than they actually were. They say women, in general, have poor self image because of what is expected of them. Why don't men, in general, have poor self image because of all those jokes they hear about penis size, baldness, being too short, bad in bed? Maybe some men deal with their poor self image by kicking women out of casinos with their hands on their asses. You can apply the word, whore, to a man but it just sounds funny, amusing. The sting is gone for some reason. This city doesn't pretend otherwise. That's right, this is the most sincere place on earth. Nobody is pretending to not be trying to not think about something other than nothing here. They are obviously trying to not think about something. And yes, it is acceptable here to want to be very thin and beautiful. This city, if it were only one man, would be a man who says out loud to women things most men know not to say out loud. And all the people in this city, if they were all only one woman, would be a woman who can often appreciate a man who doesn't beat around the bush. This gives the people of this city an opportunity to be themselves. Just like that show. Remember that show? It was amazing. It was amazing. People climbing poles with their arms stretched out in front of them and their legs above their heads. The only body part touching the pole was their hands. Even their hands had muscles. They must have wanted to be professional gymnasts. But they are doing incredible things, while dressed as fancy chickens in neon instead. Their theme was something to do with dreams, something about believing the unbelievable. Maybe it's the same theme all the time. You didn't like that clown. You hated that clown. You wondered if they had to take turns being the clown because it seemed so incredibly degrading to have to be the clown if before you came to this city your dream was to be a professional gymnast. His job was to go around spilling popcorn on audience members, or dropping his hat on their faces, or hitting on middle aged women whose husbands are sitting next to them. People laughed. People really, actually laughed. You didn't get it. Instead it dawned on you that women bleed down there anyway. When you saw those men holding each other up with their legs split wide open you thought of how horrible it would be if they tore or ripped down there and had to see blood on that part of their body. That would be grotesque, you thought, blood coming out of that part of the body. It is such a fragile place, one that carries so much psychic weight. The sight of blood there would be unconsciously traumatizing. Then you remembered you are a woman. Immediately afterwards you remembered that when you were young you had daydreams about being a dancer, even though nothing you really are, or really want to be, is a dancer. You must have been daydreaming you were somebody else, not somebody you even have it in you to want to be, not somebody better or worse, just somebody different. Why would you do that? You were daydreaming of being a completely different person than the one you are. Maybe a boy was involved. Maybe you wanted to look beautiful in your daydreams because you liked a boy, and a girl who is not you could possibly look beautiful dancing for him. Close your eyes now. You won't miss your stop. You are really tired, you can't keep your eyes open. You have to stop staying up all night. But what you see now is better than what's actually happening around you. People everywhere sitting up, staring but not staring, pretending you are not there as they are looking at you. You can play the what color is the person and how many on the bus game. No, what you can imagine is more exciting. After all, it's only ever the in between space of not being able to imagine and not being able to really see what is right in front of you that makes the good in life disappear. But right now you still can. You can imagine. You want to announce to everybody that you are going to get down on the floor of this bus and go to sleep until this is over, because you can't keep your eyes open. In the meantime you are having these thoughts about all kinds of things. Images that you are sure someone who writes could use in one of their stories. You see amazing things that immediately after seeing, you forget that you have seen. You can't remember anything that you have thought about from one second to the next for the last few seconds. You are falling asleep. You are conceiving of individual images so incredible they could carry the psychic weight of a story on their backs. But you are happy because if you can't remember something then it must not have been that important. Don't let yourself go, you'll miss your stop. Remember all those little men? It is curious that these little men lining the street handing out cards that have naked girls on them all seem to be Mexican or something. They are all so short though and look the same. Maybe they are natives of somewhere else and have come here to work. They are so short, and they all look the same, like they're all brothers. The girls on the cards all look the same too. They could all be sisters. But you don't think they really look like that, these women on the cards. They can't possibly. But maybe they can. All these little men look the same, why can't all the blonde women with large circular breasts look the same? The little men must be making those strange noises to get people's attention. Clucking or clicking or hissing. Clucking and clicking and hissing all at once. How do they do that? As if someone will miss them. As if all of them, standing there in a row reaching out to hand everyone cards, could go unnoticed, because they are so small. They must drop all the cards on the ground and pick up a stack of new ones at some point. The street is littered with little pictures of these girls, or women. Yes, women. This way if somebody is too ashamed to take a card out of their hands, from their out stretched arms, they can look down and memorize the numbers. You can't see the numbers. You can only see blonde women with large, unnaturally circular breasts, on their knees. Remember that lady who put hairspray in your hair in the bathroom of that restaurant? The one who said she has met all those actors in her salon. She said you know you glow, without even noticing the rhyme. But then she said you have a good spirit, you know. You know what I mean? I see people. You know what I mean? I work with lots of people. When I used to do these famous people's hair . . . No, I don't. I really don't. You said angrily because you thought she was crazy. I don't think I glow. And I don't have a good spirit. Now stop touching my hair. You thought this lady has been taking in too many fumes from hair supplies to be out tonight. Then you got really happy because you realized you had learned how to live in this city. Sometimes you give homeless people money, but now you know which ones don't deserve your change. You were looking at her and thinking about how she's just one of those overly made up old women who live here now but who are probably still hicks anyway, even though she was talking about your spirit. Now you do that all the time, think mean things about people who you think are crazy. You can't ever know if everybody goes through something similar, or if it's just you. You can't compare. How could you, how do you ask somebody to explain to you the nuances of thoughts they have had? What if there were no words, you wonder. Would all your thoughts be just hurt feelings? Then you would be good, and then actually have a good spirit. People would not be overly made up hicks without those words. You stayed in this city because you thought it would be cruel not to do what somebody wanted you to do to make him happy, remember? It is not worth making somebody you love sad just so you can get to do what you want. You are sure now this makes you a kind of a good person. It makes you a kind of kind. Maybe you do have a good spirit because you are in this city and not another city. What would it have made of you anyway, a nicer city? Would it have made you a better person? Would it have made you wise? Probably not, but you could have collected some nice stories. Why would it have been good for you to have nicer stories? So you could feel like somebody nice will fall in love with you someday. I know someday you will stop wanting somebody when you realize you have gained nothing at all from wanting it so much. You would have had to cut back on the traveling to different cities anyway once you realized that nowhere you go will some male native you are attracted to show you around and have a wild passionate week, month, few months with you before you have to get back on the train, boat, plane. You would have learned things about different places though, somewhere other than here. You would have had experiences that nobody cared about, and maybe would have made some stories. Maybe before you get home tonight you should stop by that French hotel place for the buffet dinner. All that champagne alone is probably worth the thirty dollars. What is the longest somebody has stayed there? You could probably be there for hours before anybody noticed. You wonder if it's a good place to be if you're homeless, warmth and all the food you can eat. Yes, but you would have to come up with the thirty dollars you need to get in, wouldn't you? The last time you were there you couldn't enjoy it. You were tired and sad. You couldn't appreciate the buffet, the same way some people can't really enjoy one aspect of their lives, like success on the job, unless everything is fine at home, or vice versa. When everything is fine, then we can enjoy buffets, some of us, sometimes. Good don't go, just make something at home. And don't waste any money on a cab tonight either. Remember that last driver? In the city I am from we treat woman in a good way, he said. This city it is unacceptable. He was basically saying we protect women by covering them up, so that they aren't grabbed by their breasts and asses. He was basically saying women have to earn the right to not be grabbed by their breasts by covering up. You tried to explain to him that barring circumstances of war there is probably, relatively the same amount of torture and abuse of women in both cities, unfortunately. In the cab driver's cities women get raped more by relatives and don't let people know. In this city women get raped more on dates with acquaintances or by strangers waiting for them to go to their cars at night and don't let people know. In this city some make phone calls to the police and there are more films made to lament the subject matter however. All any people can do is make laws against things anyway. You can't change anything really, but the gesture makes this city better than his city. Remember when you saw a man reach out and squeeze that woman's breast while they were dancing close to the bar? She moved his hands away and kept dancing a little while longer to pretend everything was all right. Then she walked away sad. She was probably a hoochie who got in over her head. He laughed and kept dancing alone. If you have breasts then somebody you don't want to grab them might grab them someday. Because they want to, and you are weaker than they are, so they can do what they want to you. Do you remember when that kid on a bike rode up next to you at night and said hey baby. Where are you going? You smiled and said home. It wasn't a happy smile, it was an embarrassed small laugh almost. He looked like a little twelve-year-old kid, and you were much older, you had just moved to this city. He said can I come home with you. You smiled, laughed, again and said no. He reached out and squeezed your breasts. You tried to lift your arms up to stop it, but it was too late. He rode off. He looked back at you, winked and licked his lips. You were convinced that you shouldn't have smiled. You told the secretary at work the next day and she said you let him get you? Why didn't you walk faster or push him off? You were new to the city. You imagined pushing him off of his bike. You as a city girl who can run after people instead of just walking back home and thinking about why you smiled, grabbing your own breasts manically so you can get the feel of his hands off of you, replace his hands with your hands, while feeling his hands instead of your hands over and over again, every time. Years later you ran into a disgusting man you had been with, when you used to do those kinds of things. You were disgusted with yourself for ever having been with him but thought you should stay and have a drink so you don't seem unkind. While talking, waiting for the drinks to come, he suddenly turned his hands into scissors, opened his fingers wide, and ran his fingers from the base of your breasts to your nipples, and laughed. You thought you had to pretend it was all right because he had brought you a drink and everybody in the bar might have been watching anyway. It made you want to take your clothes off and slide your body across broken glass, remember? You tried to explain this feeling to the secretary at work, but all she had to say was something about how you had had sex with him. I don't understand, she said. You didn't know if it had something to do with the fact that she was born in this city. You asked a male co-worker who has been with prostitutes if he would, if he saw a prostitute later at a bar, do something like that. Would you outside of that kind of, you know, situation, see a prostitute you have been with months later and touch her breasts in public like that? He said no, but in that situation the relationship is clear. The relationship was clear in my situation too you said. He laughed. Ironically it is these minor abuses against your breasts that make you terrified walking down these streets. The major abuses against you have already been written down in your spare time. The major ones have happened to characters in movies too, dozens of characters, dozens of times. But these minor incidents do not make a story. When you get home maybe you can pour a glass of wine, light a cigarette, and write it down, the way you jotted down your feelings about smoking indoors yesterday. You don't want to smoke indoors really, but pretending that you do is important here. You don't want to realize that you can go from wanting to smoke indoors to not wanting it by just growing older. How unintentional it is to stop liking somebody, or something, you used to love, to suddenly not be the person who loved that thing anymore. You used to love smoking indoors. You didn't stop voluntarily. How could something you used to enjoy so much feel so bad now? Your eyes burn, your chest hurts from being in a room full of smoke all night. Time passed and you stopped liking something you used to enjoy. He came home one day and he didn't know how he ever did it, how he could have ever wanted to be with me, you wrote. You will go home and light a cigarette. When we all have to live indoors you will be happy because you won't have to walk down these streets and remember things. When you get home tonight you will pour a glass of wine, light a cigarette, and re-watch a movie.

THERE ARE CLINICS IN THE CITY

Well, what do you want to do about this? It is up to you.

Oh, no. I want to do this. I know I want to do it. I think I just feel ashamed.

What is it that is making you feel ashamed? Do you not use protection ever?

We did sometimes. The night that it happened we didn't. He was supposed to pull out and he didn't.

Yeah.

I just knew better. I can't believe I let this happen. I am older, and I am educated. But I am not trying to say that people who aren't educated always get pregnant when they don't want to or anything like that, but I had no excuse.

Well, I know women who come in here who are thirty years old who have families who have had kids before who still find themselves in this mess. This isn't something that happens to young people, or old people, or smart people, or stupid people. You just have to think about what you want to do about it now.

I want to do this. I know there is no way I can have it.

All right. Well the options at this point are to take a pain killer and wait, since the IV isn't going to work.

I can do the IV now. It's just always been hard to find my veins. When she said she was going to try the vein on my hands I should have told her to go for the one on the side of my wrist. That one usually works better when someone is drawing blood. I was just watching the blood drip down from my hand and I was thinking about things. I think that's all that happened.

I don't think at this point they are going to try the IV again, Honey. They won't try and use your hands again because it's more painful and it is harder to keep the IV in place. The only reason she tried your hands was because she wasn't getting blood from your arms and you said you wanted the IV, but it is not what we usually do. I think you will be fine with just a pain killer. We wait twenty minutes to make sure it has kicked in so that you are more relaxed and calm. That's usually all it takes.

Does it take away the actual pain?

No, the Vicodin won't work on the actual nerve endings but it will just relax you and make you not as interested in the pain.

There is no way to knock me out?

No, I'm sorry, Honey. There is no way to do that. That way we can stay a clinic. That is why this is just a clinic. We wouldn't be able to do what we do if this were a hospital. We can't do anything that requires that much medical attention. And we don't feel it's necessary, to be honest. The entire procedure takes a few minutes. We don't really feel it requires sedation.

All right. Well, I'll just do the painkiller then. But I don't think it will work really well on me. It usually takes a lot of painkillers to work on me, like when I have cramps or something. I have to take four or five Aleves before I feel any better.

Well, Vicodin is much different than other painkillers you would get over the counter. I could ask them if she will give you two. Will that make you feel better?

Yeah, thank you. That might help.

I could also be in the room with you to hold your hand if you would like.

You don't have to.

No, don't worry about it. That's what I'm here for.

Thank you. I'm sorry about this. I'm not usually like this.

I know it's a hard thing to go through. What you should do is make sure you vote. There are people trying to take away your right to this.

Why aren't there two? Barbara said you could give me two.

That's not what we usually do. Usually one is enough. Do you want me to go talk to her?

No, that's all right.

All right. So, you just need to take your pants off in the back there and lie down.

Barbara said she was going to be here.

Go get Barbara.

There you are!

Can I talk to you for a second, Barbara?

So why does she want you in here?

The poor girl just came back from vacation and found out she was pregnant. After the ultrasound they tried to give her the IV and she nearly passed out. I told her I would be in here to hold her hand.

All right. Let's get this over with.

Ok. How are you doing? Good. Now put your legs up on the stirrup. Good. Now up further. Good. Thank you. I will be telling you what will happen as I am doing it, so you are not nervous. So just relax. I will tell you what I will be doing as I am doing it. Oops, sorry. I am going to first take a look so you will feel a pinch first, then some pressure from these things that look like pliers here. I am going to start out by placing them in your vagina, then I am going to open them up so I can get a better look. All right. Now. Once I do that I will stick this thing, that looks like a straw, inside you to irritate the lining of the uterus. You are actually so early on that I can just use the pump, and we don't have to use the vacuum. So that's good. So, after I irritate the lining I will place this in your vagina and suck the lining out. All right. So let's get started this should only take a minute. All right I am going in now to irritate the lining, so you will feel some pain.

Just hold my hands, Sweetie.

Now I am going in with the pump.

Breathe. Just breathe. Keep breathing. That's right.

All right that was good. You're doing good. Now just one more time. Just one more time.

Just to make sure we have got everything out. This will just take a second.

It's almost over.

All right that's it. We are all done.

All right, there will be bleeding. Do you want me to help you up? All right. I am handing you a pad right here. Can you get up? There will be some bleeding, so you want to put the pad on. How do you feel?

It did hurt.

Really?

It really hurt.

Really? Well, they will prescribe more Vicodin for you if you want. You can take some more painkillers for tonight. They will tell you what you need to do. You know, not to pick things up and to get a lot of rest.

Thank you.

TO THE SHELTER

There is in them the scent of the decease of their owners in spite of all the new fashions. In all their array they make the city really like a new thing rather than the last surviving results of the more burdensome adornments of the past. It is only their walls who seem to cry out during the delicate times the city suffers. It is also only their very walls who insinuate music to make conversation. This timbre is more than known to their inhabitants, and is likely to be constantly unearthed. The buildings converse widely and assure the people of the city, of the city, where people toil for long hours. The city is like its carpenters and its brick layers. The walls of this or that building are employed for the city's fair arrangement. The buildings themselves are a piece of concrete music and in part add to the sense of solid harmony. All the while the people sleep the pale green and little blue touches on the buildings dance. Also the buildings make it necessary to confess that this city is a hard won place. Instead of being merely the furniture of ancestors, the buildings are the shade and shelter. They have come together much against the inclinations of fathers and mothers who have advised against them. The whole city is one painting, a portrait in the vast and fortuitous massing of light and shadow. Its buildings are wont to permit themselves the freedoms of the lines and textures. Around the buildings the trees are suspended with their wonderful blithesomeness. Only the gods and the charms of their works can understand this architecture. Though this would be the people's last preference, for the buildings to be the world in which they pass their lives, to be struck only by the purity of these structures the city has furnished. There is sweetness yet in the form and color of things, in the actual life to which they hope to run. It is true that the city relishes in the pure and strong, the pit of their work. The buildings are akin to some other objects which perish or vanish in the city. These offices of religion are always a sight to behold here. Never are the gods actually seen, but they are much more desired as sight to behold. In its cathedrals a certain world has come from afar to give its blessing to the city with infinite delicacy. The people have come from afar to see god, and hear him mouth silently in their city. The people are grateful for the movement of his hands which they feel in the grand, closed air that fills the cathedrals. Here they can refine their souls. They are permitted to be old, to impress, to be genuine, and to honor even in their disappointments with a natural grace. They gather to see statues to see how god is like their city, a hard structure without seams. They congregate in an ornate cage for one who might have made them, so that he bestows his portrait on his remains. These gifts that forge and heave could not be endured outside god's presence. They pay homage here to their hard hearted and difficult friend. Outside of the cathedral they could not endure his presence. Outside of the cathedral they become a herd heated by all things difficult. They fancy themselves a congregation that must converge. And at times they become together like one child having found one day a timely box in which to place his thoughts. They piece together the money in their hands and give it to the servers. This money that comes into their hands can excite and open their days and nights. The money can break the last sip of mirth and drive away the rattling of misery's coaches. They speak across tables with laughter on their lips, or with bitter tears in their eyes. They understand everything that matters to this delicate life here. They speak so expectantly, with so much spirit, partly because after all they have endured they have flown to this place. What is upon them, or despised by them, they persuade themselves is a satisfaction of their present means. All the while they indulge in their apparent preferences and their vain coquetries. These perishable graces of wine, of food, can be rendered so perfectly only through an intimate understanding of themselves. They understand that these nourishments must be desired and earned to be enjoyed by them in pure happiness. Still, they have everything to do, yet for the moments their only realized intention is to imbibe, is to consume. They have their most preferred locations, and this must give them the sense, the thought, of independence. They have purchased their time here and so can escape from one languid day to another, just as it may please them. Here they have already seated somewhat the anxiety of their day more than once or more than twice. They leave thinking, after all in all we are in the great world. The rewards that lie on a table before them are now greatly a part of them. This gap is now bridged to enter and they certainly want to relish. They are always half in expectation for these visits. The sorrows expressed before these memorials which were engraved with names in sand with dates of the deceased are shaped here in the form of silence. It is relief now that carves the quiet spaciousness and acts as a recollection to clear ways for the condition of the heart. Outside the cemeteries' gates one can suppose that the clouds folding on the metal coaches, the sound of individual footsteps, and the routes thrust into existence are standing near. The constant odor of this or that dead earth is prevalent as a reminder. Small old ants walk along the paths atop small old people. There are no lights here to help the cemetery show its people. They visit this place on certain nights, though they do not stay. In a preoccupied manner, it is true the same very one of their successes is dependent on, they do not want to burden the cemeteries' residents with life. What can the gone understand of the styles, what can be taken into account of the still beating kind head, the pensive solid heart. The living's place is to appoint, or decorate, or shame these rooms with only windows. Only the first flood of thought occupies. These cemeteries become landmarks in time. They think of old fashions and indulge in the contrasts between what is living and what is dead. The cemeteries' residents live in the deep brown, with white bottomless days, without shadow in cool and pleasant confinement. They have brought themselves in from the cutting sunshine of their own country. They make this their city, where their needs must be economized, where it is not the shade, but rather the sun whose weight clamps a little on one's dissolved spirits. Outdoors the many wheels of the city are spinning. These moving fixtures so daintily woven mark the terrain. Inside the cafes there is sanctuary from something felt by the visitors long ago. Here it interests them to honor the ancient traditions. The young man and the young woman, the homely old man and old woman, leave the rudeness of their home to speak about the weather. They have turned to this city to know the ever slimming graces of life. This fluid becomes something turned into a physical want like a thunder, or a thirst. They greet each other with might. They come to greet here, what perhaps can overwhelm. There is something here that some think is a hard fate. It is in an offensive place where their feet must touch only one ground. When they can no longer sketch on the wind the half strides of their thoughts, when the pavement takes on another torrent, the people who cannot stay home travel to this place where the only sound from without is the creaking of restless metal coaches shuttering on their hinges. They march across the place of those soldiers coming and going, one hardly knows whether to or from a battle in a sleepy place, sleepier than ever since it beckons and ceases to stay near, the frontier where the cement is growing deep and old. It is a pleasant walk there and musing where one can muse about pleasant thoughts in the minds of those inside the metal coaches. They amuse themselves here. Here a scene is painted that they have known forever to be true of other places. Here they emerge from their work, they depart in company, they offer fine threaded thoughts to the trees free to sway. For several months a year the park is ruffled with foliage. Since they have gone, but not come back this way of nature, it is at times the only way to be chosen. They walk in these cheap portraits of another reality, or fantasy, to expose themselves to the air. They receive for their pain a thing for their soul. How I delight myself in fanciful gardens. Trimmed yet less stiffly worn than those around all of our other houses. They come to see the trees when the summer days are over or when they begin. They enjoy the shade of foliaged trees, each of them with a corner of inbuilt country, and beyond over which the sun is sinking. Their thoughts have been returned to them here. This part of this city has proven itself with a character so independent that all things become well. They stay with each tree here instead of their houses full of old people and young people. Suppose they come for themselves so they can say, we have become, we have seen the streets, so scrupulous, are not all the city has to offer? Yes, the trees here can take care of us with their neatness. The people are lovers of distinction and elegance. They can trace these lines like the bloom of a flower and say there are god's things here. There are attractive things in life meant for one not for another, not meant for those people. They are meant, perhaps, for us, as there are trees which are not suitable for every one. There is the discourse of these paintings in the crushes of these buildings. These worlds are full and rich and simple standing firmly on either side present with old homely people to look at with the attitude of ones amidst glory. Set here in the frames are openings of a garble of plates, of flowers, of all feeling. Everything is finished except a grating opulence, the robes of shadowy blue shutters. The frame around canvas is a better fare than the hold of flesh. In spite of their amplitude, the paintings carry a royal ease of action under their stiff coarse costumes. There are people returned from an early mass. They come here to where life lingers long after the offices were ended and watch pondering the hours of the world. One of them could help a small butterfly which has landed on the canvas, but could find no way out again. It will, they suspect, remain there to flutter round and round distractedly far up under the arched roof of frame until forever so it never dies vanquished. They come to see what has been made by the twitter and whirl manipulated by a man's hands. Here is a bird passing jotting once only on some winter night from window to window across a cheerfully lightened hall, forever the painter's captive. It was taken captive by the ill luck of the moment it orbited around his thoughts, until it expired within the closet of frame and canvas. This vaunting child is designated exclusively to this place. This is all in order that the city becomes a particular kind of parchment. They must not underrate this great gift. The movement towards a seemingly fleeting happiness is not on the hem of these tracks. It is in them so much as to move them. It is judged too much by the contrast between the delicate life outside the train and the squares and cubes inside it. They are now to leave and go to another city. And so among the trees outside the windows of the trains are houses, buildings, restaurants, cafes, cemeteries, museums. The unrefined and refined throw away, the bald existence of theirs in this the old city. They are agitated by what is really disclosed below such a speedy surface. So this is how one cures the incurable wanderlust one is not supposed to nature. That old city, that delightful old place that has lost its modesty and grown into only buildings, green and blue and weather stained. They have known it all their lives. Inside these high whitewashed walls they ate and drank and exploded in their mirth. They stared out large windows inside buildings opposite which there were yards and parks in the summertime. On the train is the wonderful stir of color and sound in the wide open space beneath the smaller windows. Their eyes are sketching the scenes of life, but with a kind of grace, a marvelous tact of omission. How is the train dealing with the vulgar reality seen from one's own, seen as people in some fairyland see, or some clever tragic world that for the humor of the thing has put on motley and been able to be forsaken . . .

BUSY BARS

"So, I went into that really busy bar on Twelfth Street. The one you and I used to go to every once in a while when we lived on Pleasant. What is it called, the Naked Horse, or Bull, or something? I hated that place, but it was snowing and the street was empty and I was so depressed because Collin hadn't called. Anyway, the place was crowded as usual, so I got a drink at the bar and looked around for somewhere to stand. There were these two guys sitting at that little table, the one by the jukebox. I went over with my drink and stood behind them. I don't know what made me do it. I saw their elbows resting on the dark worn wood that is all over that place and it just seemed right somehow. You wouldn't think, would you? Just two guys in t-shirts and jeans with beer in their hands and now I feel better. They weren't even that good looking, it wasn't anything like that. So I ordered a gin and tonic and walked towards them and stood facing the alligator sign that says Bud Light in the middle. So let's just pretend one of them is named John and the other one is named Joe. They were talking about work, I think, and the one named John says something like, he's actually a pretty nice guy once you get to know him. And the one named Joe says something like, yeah, I liked hanging out with him that night. Then John says his sense of humor is pretty awkward. I don't know what he's going for sometimes, whether he's pissed off or not. Then Joe says Kim is like that sometimes too. She would call me an asshole or something and I would just laugh it off most of the time, but sometimes I think . . . Then John asks, where is she now? Joe says, she's going back home this week. It's over. I am tired of her games. Having to fucking figure out what she wants to hear when she wants to hear it, and dealing with how fucking crazy she would get when . . . And John says something like yeah, that sucks man. But Joe wants to keep talking about it. He starts getting really serious and says I just couldn't handle it anymore, man. John obviously didn't want to talk about it. He says something like maybe now you can concentrate on those reports. He was really fucking angry when you handed him that shit without . . . Now Joe is really mad and says I don't know what the fuck his problem was . . . You gotta admit that he had a right to be . . . They went on like this about work for a while until Joe looked like he was going to cry or something. His voice was strained and chalky at times trying to finish some of his sentences. I felt really bad for him. That's when I realized that Collin is sad about us right now too. Just because he didn't call doesn't mean he is not upset. I feel really bad for him because he has nobody to talk to. I know he can sometimes talk to Jake, but Jake only lets him talk for so long before he changes the subject and starts talking about himself. I never understood why they were friends in the first place. But I guess Collin feels a loyalty to him since they have known each other for so long. He's like that, he's a really loyal friend. Anyway, I finished my drink and went to get another one. When I came back they were talking about some party at work, or something like that. I couldn't hear everything because of how loud it gets in that place, but John said something like, he must be doing something right. I couldn't believe it when he showed up with her. And Joe says you know she's fucking his money. I don't know, man, but she's hot, he's lucky. You really think a girl like that would be with him if he weren't fucking loaded? You never know. He's pretty . . . Kim is the only woman I know that doesn't care about that shit. She . . . What the fuck are you talking about you were always bitching about how she . . . We never fought about money . . . Anyway, that girl was hanging off . . . But Joe was already defensive at this point. We fought about where to go, or what to do with money, but she didn't care whether or not I have money.

John wasn't really listening, I don't think. He would just look down at his beer, pick up the glass, and take a big gulp occasionally. He turned his head away from Joe and pretended to look very interested in what was going on around him. He must not have wanted to be rude though, because by the time I had come back with another drink I think he had pointed out a girl standing at the bar and was talking about her breasts or something. Probably to let Joe know that they can still have a decent night. Joe just nodded his head. He agreed about her breasts, but he didn't really seem interested. She's too fucking tall, Joe said.

They are all the same height when they are lying down.

Yeah, whatever, there's no way . . .

You should go talk to her, she's drunk enough.

Kim actually liked how short I was. She actually said that . . .

That's when I realized that they both must not be very tall. I couldn't really tell before since they were sitting down. Maybe they were brothers and that's why they are both about five foot six or five foot seven or eight inches tall. They kind of had short legs, but you know how you can't really tell. But they work together too. Anyway, I realized that Collin must have had some of these same insecurities. It must be really hard for men. They have to approach women and wonder whether or not they will be rejected all the time. When Collin and I first met we didn't have to go through any of that uncomfortable stuff. We became friends first. But that's when I realized that so much of what we fought over had to do with his insecurities still. He must have wondered constantly whether or not I really loved him, whether or not he was good enough for me. That's when I began to see everything clearly. I saw these two squeezed out lime slices lying on top of each other on the floor as I walked over to the bar. It almost looked as if they were holding each other, lying helplessly on each other like that. Their pulp was ruffled and furry and such a bright green. And when I got back I saw the rings on their table, the water rings left from the glasses. I noticed how the table was a circle and the coasters were only circles and the rings . . . I can't explain why, but I knew then that Collin and I are going to come back to each other. All the fighting is part of a cycle, a circle, we go through to get back to each other. I could hear Joe say, she told me that at first she thought about it, but then as we got to know each other she even started feeling uncomfortable around tall guys. She started feeling awkward when a tall guy got close to her, to try and hug her or something, because it felt like there was all this space between them. She really liked how we were at eye level . . . Then he started saying something about how Kim would have these crazy dreams when she fell asleep drunk that he wished he had written down. He thought she had the strangest, most beautiful, dreams. That's how I felt about Collin. I wanted to record what he said sometimes. I wanted to count how many times he did certain things. Everything that bothered me about how he looked or how he dressed at first became the only way a man should look or dress after a while.

I noticed that John had a blank look on his face, but he was staring at Joe still. He must not have wanted it to be a bad night but he wasn't being a very good friend. He looked like he wanted the night to be over, but he wanted it to end on a good note. I just don't think he could understand how much Joe loved Kim. Then this girl wearing a red tank top, in the middle of winter, bumped into Joe and almost spilled her drink on his head. This actually seemed to come as a welcome surprise to John who looked up at her and laughed, then looked at Joe so they could both laugh about it. Joe said something like, somebody needs to be cut off. She looks like she's about to ask one of her friends to hold her hair back for her. Joe said Kim used to do shit like that all the time. It got fucking annoying. I knew she needed to blow off some steam every once in a while but it got to the point where I couldn't relax because I knew she was going to . . . But John cut him off with yeah, I better call it a night. I need to get some sleep for . . . I knew that John and Joe were going to leave soon, so . . ."

A young dark haired waiter carrying a tray of glasses puts down a margarita and two glasses of water on their table and waits. Mary looks up at him smiling. She puts the menu she has been staring into down by the chips and salsa.

"Are you ready to order?" Mary says.

"Yeah sure. Basically, I realized that when Collin said that . . ."

"Do you want to look at the menu? We should order soon."

"I'll just give you more time," the waiter says smiling as he walks away.

Mary's eyes follow the waiter. Liz picks up the menu with one hand and the margarita with the other. She looks up at Mary and begins speaking hurriedly as Mary looks down at the menu.

"Basically, I understood why he thought we couldn't stay together. His thoughts must have come crashing in on him after one of our fights and he didn't know what to do to make things better. He is probably trying to forget about me right now. Before last night I felt like that was a sign that he never loved me as much as I loved him. But everybody can make themselves forget anything they want to really. It's easy enough. It doesn't mean anything. It certainly doesn't mean lack of love. If anything, it probably means that you are really, really in love if what is going on with another person is hurting you to the point where you need to forget about them. People that don't let go of things just don't really want to let go. But he must be so hurt that he's trying to let go. I just put too much pressure on him to remember things, to be a certain way sometimes. Lately I have been thinking about all the other men that have been in my life and how it is really all right now that they are gone. But I just don't think I will ever feel that way about Collin. All the laughing and talking we did, that was really just about him, about us. I have tried to fantasize about better looking, more sophisticated men, but it's all really about wanting to look at someone. So for me there is nobody better looking than Collin is because I don't want to stare at anybody's face except his. I know that we never really know if what we are feeling is real in the moment, or if anything will last, since things don't sometimes, even when we think they will. It's not worth thinking about what could have been if it probably wouldn't have been if we stayed together, so I really can't have any good memories of somebody if everything would have turned bad anyway. But after last night, I know I love him. I know I could try and make it work again. I know it would be different. I would be different. You know how they say you can only see ten percent of an iceberg because most of it is under water? Well, Collin is an iceberg to me. His mind, his heart, he is an iceberg only I can see all of. You know, when you just have to know somebody because of the way they smile, or the way they touch only you, or call just at the right time. Collin makes me believe in spiritual connections. He makes me believe in magic. How else could I have laughed so hysterically sometimes that I couldn't even remember where I was anymore if there wasn't something real between us? I got to the point where everything I did with anybody was about him and what he would think of me. That was the mistake I made. I lost the independence he loved so much about me. It is what ruined our relationship. It's like when you are doing a juice fast and at first . . ."

Mary turns her head to stare at the Coronita Extra bottles filled with salt and pepper next to the sugar container. She looks at Liz briefly then turns her head away again. She takes out a couple of the pink sugar packets, shakes them, then puts them down by the menu. At the table behind them a little boy and a little girl are fighting over a glass of water. Mary turns her head to stare.

There are some things that can only happen in the city.

Well, if you are a woman, or a man, you can be hit on by men with all kinds of accents. You can see if different kinds of men would be willing to tell you they think you are beautiful. In a bar that caters to white women who are looking for Arab men you can even find one with a word shaved on the back of his head. You could also open a restaurant in a very trendy area of the city if you have the money. A place where alcohol is very expensive but also where bartenders enjoy giving the occasional customer a free drink, even when they don't ask for a second one or a third one, so they buy a fourth one. Make sure to make the music in the background only loud enough so they can hear it and hear each other. Name this restaurant Joe's or Jack's, something short and simple. Make it look like a place anybody would be welcome but charge enough for the food so as to attract the passerby, as well as the moneyed patron. Hire all male waiters, and make sure they are very attractive, so that women are happy to be served by them, and men are happy that they are being served by them. Occasionally make the customer think they are getting a discount by letting them know about the discount menu where prices are the same as they would be if you didn't have the word discount on the menu. You can make this restaurant your whole life if you wanted. And maybe someday on your way home you will witness a large riot, the kind that can only happen in a city.

There are things that can only happen in the city.

Today on the bridge she saw herself. She was a small fly looking up in intricate webs made of steel. She was small above and below a world made of sharp hot edged metals. When she went home. She took a bath. She pulled herself out of the tub, went to the phone naked and wet, sat on the carpet, and just dialed. She did this again and again changing only one number each time. She tried to explain something to someone mumbling for a little while until each one hung up. She wants to say I love you every time, but didn't. Their voices each contained all forms of palpable weather. Sunshine whines and raindrop wheezes and snowflakes and scalding cold winds. Then she dialed again, changing only one of the numbers.

The woman who misses the man in another city thinks about the things that can only happen in the city.

If I will die alone then it will be in his city. His city is bigger than my city. There I can walk and see all the people. I can go to restaurants alone where I can eat food that is the best food to eat alone or with people. I can go see films and plays anytime of the night or day because there is always someplace open in the city. If I am going to die alone I will only have a body to feed and watch things inside of. If I have to be alone in a room then I want to be alone in a room in his city where I can hear the people and watch people outside through a window.

There are things that can only happen in the city.

The city teaches its people how to be smart enough to live on its streets. It teaches them how to live in the city. It makes them the resourceful animals of the city. They will not let you harm them. They are accustomed to how things are done in the city. They are accustomed to seeing the homeless and so they are not afraid of them. They give the homeless money, sometimes, but they know which homeless people don't deserve their change now. The city has taught them who is and who is not a liar. If you want you can come here and sell your paintings. You can sell maps to the city. You can sell maps to the parks of the city. You can sell ice cream to the people walking into the parks.

There are things that can only happen in the city.

You can go into a large hotel, the largest and most expensive in the city, only to sit at the bar of the hotel, the only place where a rare merlot is served. You can order this wine from a waitress who does not know you are lonely, who thinks you are on a business trip and have a family in another city. She may bring you complimentary bread and butter which will be the best bread and butter not made in the city that you can buy only in the city. If you smell something sweet on the waitress, you can ask her what it is. If it is an unusual perfume that can only be purchased in one store in the city. You can buy it. If you want to smell her again you can finish the glass of wine and go to this store next to the hotel to buy her rare perfume.

There are things that can only happen in the city.

If you are willing to plan ahead and make a reservation you can eat next to one of the richest men in the city. On your way to your car you can give one of the poorest men in the city your change.

There are all kinds of people living in the city.

One woman says to her children get back get back these mother fuckers are crossing. Can't you see? What the fuck are you doing?

A minute later one woman asks her children what do we do when we cross the street, that's right, we look both ways. What color is the light? That's right. What does that mean? That's very good. You're doing fine.

Then a man looks at a young girl as they cross the intersection in opposite directions and yells out what's your name, you have a pretty smile. What was that? Mary, well, when you see me again you can have whatever you want, Mary. Every time you see me you just ask for whatever you want. The girl thinks there are so many of them out today. There must be a game at the stadium or something. Or maybe there are always this many of them in the center of the city but I just hadn't noticed.

Then a young man begging on the street asks a woman if he can have a cigarette, at least, since she walked past his outstretched hands without giving him money. She rolls her eyes and gives him her cigarette. The woman gives the young man the cigarette out of her mouth. Just takes it out of her mouth and gives it to him because he asked. Then she rolls her eyes and looks sick as she walks away.

Then a man starts screaming at the other men waiting for the train. He says I heard you say *that black guy*. I heard you say it when I walked by, don't fucking lie to me, I heard you talking. Fuck you. I heard it. *That black man.*

Then a man says to a woman who is carrying a bag full of movies I guess it's a Blockbuster night tonight, right? It's a Blockbuster night tonight. She is embarrassed by this. She thinks of what he must be trying to say about her. She thinks about how she could be somebody with a family for all he knows. She could be watching movies with her family. She thinks about why these people feel comfortable saying things like that to her out loud. She thinks about how what he said is an invasion of her privacy. She thinks about how they think it's shameful to watch so many movies because they do drugs and think their drugs are more interesting than her movies.

There are all kinds of people in the city.

Fucking excuse you.

You fucking four eyed honky.

Fuck you, you fucking four eyed geek.

You made me drop my phone, you fucking honky.

White boy piece of shit.

Fuck you.

You made me break my phone, you fucking four eyed bitch.

There are all kinds of people living in the city.

I don't drink and drive.

That's smart.

My friend say why you don't drink and drive? I say them, because I not stupid like you.

Yeah, that's a good idea, it's dangerous.

You don't know when you will die.

That's true you never know what will happen from one day to the next.

From one day, no, not even from one second you don't know.

That's true.

We could be a homeless too.

Yup, you never know.

We have to be kind with each other. You know, they don't know I ride bus.

Well, that's a good secret.

I don't tell my wife and my son. But one man on the bus say to me I won't shake your hand, you are Mooslem. But, I am not. Why he say that to me?

He must have assumed, I suppose.

We all equal, every man.

That's true.

If you come to my restaurant you see how they respect you. You tell them you know me.

I will do that.

I am very happy to be talking to you. You give them my name.

Yes, nice conversation makes for a good evening.

I am bothering you?

No, no I just have to watch out for these cars, some people don't know how to drive. They will get in front of a big bus like this.

I know, I know. I don't drink and drive.

There are all kinds of people living in the city.

Step right up to the magic show.

Ladies and gentlemen.

It's fun and easy, like my last girlfriend.

It lasts only a few minutes, like the man she left me for.

Step right up.

There are all kinds of people living in the city.

I got to make my sales, baby.

There are all kinds of people living in the city.

I like your shirt. Vampires do rock.

I know if they were real I would let one of them bite me.

I know, me too.

There are all kinds of people living in the city.

Shoe shine.

Shoe shine.

People wearing slippers and sandals are shoe player haters.

There are all kinds of people living in the city.

How are you, Ms. Pretty?

Girl, you're not going to stop and talk to me for a while?

You don't talk to me no more?

All right, be like that.

I like to watch you go anyway.

Why is the city so beautiful?

The concrete is hard and so makes walking easy. The trees are chained so they are not dangerous to the people. Each place has its sign. All of the city's places are marked somehow. Though the city's streets are marked it is too big to know all of its places by heart. Like a human face, you can recognize the city but never really know how the city will change. But the signs are still and bright and tell the people where to go. The cars stop and then move again all at once all together. People can buy coffee and tea and other warm drinks at night and in the morning in places where there are signs to let them know they can buy coffee and tea. They walk on the concrete in the heart of the city with their warm water. This concrete is the city's skin. Somebody has spit on every inch of this concrete. The city allows them to do this.

Why is the city beautiful?

The moon and the sun are beautiful to the people because they create a light. Likewise, the city is beautiful because it is made of lights. The city is an unnatural beauty. The people are like insects that are attracted to light. The city is made up of insects that light up at night. The lights of the city are not like the light of the moon, or the light of the sun. They are unnatural like the city. The city is beautiful because of the lights and the unnatural shapes of its buildings. The buildings have been drawn and etched out to look unnatural to the people. Intricate, ornate buildings are beautiful to the people. When the people say the city is beautiful they are speaking of the lights and the buildings. The city is like a woman who wears makeup at night. The men of the city take women who wear make up at night to buildings that light up. When the sun is out, the city looks tame like a woman kneeling on four limbs. The city is a barefaced woman sleeping in the morning. In the morning the men and women go to buildings where they must work. In the morning the city looks tame. The men can use their arms to make and have the city every morning.

Why is the city beautiful?

The city is beautiful because there are so many people in its center who do not have buildings to go into at night. They are sprinkled all over the city. The whole city is their one home. Though people need buildings for shelter the city will keep those who do not have buildings to turn to, it will have them anyway. Some people do not have shelter but the city still provides for them. These, the homeless of the city, can use thrown away paper to make blankets and walls. These people know that when the lights of the city are set against the dark frame of the night sky, nothing is more beautiful. They sometimes think to themselves this is a city of fire and ice, a heaven where flame cannot burn you, or blow out in wind.

Why is the city beautiful?

When it starts to snow more and more people go home to turn on the lights in their buildings until the only light in the city comes from the buildings. The snow diffuses the lights to make the city look like it is encased in a heavy glass. Smoke spins out of the city as the people walk slowly in the snow. The cars move slowly too and the snow beneath them sloshes. The cars move like heavy slugs creating a gushing sound. In the snow some of the people are happy, they have somewhere to go. They sometimes think to themselves only in my city does the snow make so much noise. Only in the city does the snow not fall silently, but makes everything so silent. Once they realize that only in the city can they hear the snow under the tread of so many tires they immediately understand that the blood of the people who have died building their bridges is still in the bridges and towers and spires. Bridges made of intricate, lovely iron lace to make them like iron curtains. Then they realize that the city is the book the people wrote together. The city is their one story. That's why they made these snow covered statues to last forever.

the city is beautiful

its buildings, buildings so big that the people could not completely destroy them in the wars when the bombs killed most of the people

Why is the city beautiful?

You know, there are so many people in the city. People will not know you are alone, if you pretend, they will not know you are lonely. And maybe you will have a home here until you find a home. The city is the only place that will keep you until your fate changes, or if you have tempted your fate. That is why its slums are full of people who would otherwise have nowhere else to go. Where else would the homeless have a home except in the city? The trees of the forest and the swamps of the jungles do not protect and keep the people.

The woman in the city who misses the man in another city travels to the man's city.

My city is smaller than your city, but it is just like a big city. There is a woman here walking around passing out little pieces of paper to strangers that say Jesus loves you. Jesus cries tears of blood for your salvation. He is returning soon. And on the back, or the front, of that little piece of paper it asks you if you are ready for the coming of the Lord. It is a smaller city, but the people in my city are as different as the people in yours and this makes them just like people you will find in big cities. An old man in a wheelchair sits here on a corner in front of a stand to hold music he has made. If you give him money he will give you his music. I can kiss his hands as if he were my father or grandfather. I could know him and love him or show him things, be good to him if I wanted. I will not know him because my city is smaller than yours, but it is still a city. This city is large enough that you can find people with all kinds of shades of skin color and ages, women and men with children, putting their hands out for my money. I want to see you in this city with me. I want to walk with you. But you are not here to do that for me. I think about how I would have never treated you unkindly. It would only confuse me to see you. It will make me want you more when you reach out and touch the hands of these people asking for your money. It will make me want to see you drive past them skillfully. We would go to a restaurant and you would stare too long as our funny blonde waitress walks away. I want to be a funny blonde waitress. I want to be the waitress you love in the city you love. I want to bring you food. I want to be this blonde waitress in this city. I want her breasts and her stomach, however they may be. I want to have her feet and her laugh and her voice so that you don't have to pretend my feet are good enough for you only because I am the one sitting next to you and not the waitress. You could only appreciate my face for so long without wanting the peace of being able to stare at this waitress. I will leave this city.

The woman travels to the man's city.

You cannot tell how people will speak by the look of their faces or the look of their clothes in this city. A man may look like he is not a native of this city, but he may be a native of this city, because this city is so big you cannot ever judge its natives by what they are wearing or what they look like. It is in how they move. This beautiful girl with brown skin has very worn clothes that are not well made and dirty and she may be a native of this city as well. This man with black skin you think is too tall too be a native of this city, but he may have been born here and speak as if he knows this city too. This old almond eyed woman stares out awkwardly at nothing in the sky as she waits for the train. She makes sounds with her mouth and nose that she does not seem to know she is making. She could be from this city. Her father could be white or black or yellow. She could speak only one language or two or many. There are other cities where people look the same but are still different. The people in those cities may be poor or rich, young or old, and they each have a color. This is your big city. The train carries so many people, the train carries stairs inside it. It is a train that travels very fast and very quickly. The people on the train will sleep, or they will read. This city is so big, you cannot judge who will sleep or who will read just by looking at them. A very large woman in a stained flower print shirt will open a heavy book. A man in a suit will rest his head against the window like a child. All the people on the train are tired. Outside the windows there are fences that separate the tracks from the roads where the houses rest. There are trees on those roads but not very many. There are houses and cars outside those houses. Every station you stop at has signs advertising things that can be done and bought in the city. And on this train right now there is someone who would take all the money you have saved to travel here, the money you put in the bag next to your feet. There are so many people on this train that it is certain there is someone here who would cut you with a knife for that money. You want to believe you know who would and who wouldn't just by looking at them, but this city is too big for you to judge people by looking. It is just big enough for you to want to think you can. Houses and trees and houses and trees and houses. Cars of different colors moving away and towards the train. What can you buy in the city? The signs say a house, a gym in your house, coffee, an operation at a clinic, a mattress to sleep on in your house, a seat at a play. The train stops. One tree. Its limbs sway from side to side. Its individual leaves spin around themselves in circles all at once. Above the city is the sky. These are the smutty trees of the big city. The buildings block the wind in one direction and bring it to another. The leaves, way above on the highest branches, are always dirty until it rains. This is the natural beauty of the city. If you rest your face on the window and keep your eyes up at the sky you see the natural beauty that is the city. If you do not look down at the signs, in front of the two men getting out of their cars yelling, you think this city is beautiful. I live in this big city and you have hurt my car they may be screaming. How will I drive now to the places I need to go to buy the things I need to buy? The things you now know you can buy from staring at the signs are pills to help you sleep, a ticket for a seat at a theatre, a lamp to put next to your bed, a bed to put in your house, a house, and the trees to plant in its yard. A child on the train is crying. Why do people bring their children to the big city? Because the children were born here, they are from the big city. They are going to grow big in the city. The people make the children because they are here already. They need to eat because they are here and so feel they want to eat so they can live. They work all day before they get on the train so they can make money so they can buy the food to eat. They don't know why they work all day only so they can buy food just so they can eat just so they can keep living. So they make the children. The children give them a reason to have to work, so they can buy food, so their children can eat so their children do not die in the city.

The woman travels to the man's city.

I will leave him a message. Hi, the city is only interesting without you. I am back in your city, but you are not here with me. No. Hi, the city is only interesting without you. I promise I will be normal, and not cry, if you see me here now. No. I promise I will not touch you or cry about anything if we can have one more day in the city. No. Hi. This city, it is only interesting without you. This city is only interesting without you.

A woman travels to a man's city.

The city was only interesting and dirty without you. I would like to see you again before I leave. No. I won't be able to see you again if you don't see me today. Please come see me again then we never have to see each other again. No. The city is only interesting and dirty without you. No.

The woman who misses the man travels to his city.

The last time I missed you this very much was the day after the day we spent in this city.

The woman travels to the man...

. . . Other signs in your city say:

I am struglin'

Have Not Worked For A Year

Veteran

will work

will do anything

you can just buy me food if you think I will buy BOOZE

Please Help

Family trying to

Get back home

Anything would Help

Help me!

Yes, this will help me forget you. Your city will help me forget you. One building here has one hundred windows, maybe more, maybe hundreds of windows. I cannot tell, it is too big. A man is selling bad pastries in a cart that some people buy because they are too busy to walk a little further to the shop where good pastries are sold. You can sell good things and bad things in this city, people are in such a hurry. There are homeless people in a hurry here too. They speak to themselves and walk alone. There are people here who will ask for money to buy things so they can live. One building has only a few very large windows. One building has a large bottle of tequila painted on it. The homeless people live under this building. They cannot buy this bottle with your money. But they can buy the can of beer painted on the other building.

The woman travels to the man's city.

A man in a bar tells me it is all right that I have not found anywhere else to go on this street except this bar. He says there are not very many of certain kind of restaurants on this street in this city. But if you walk a little bit this way you will find a bookstore that sells books that cannot be sold anywhere else in the world. And if you walk that way you can eat food that cannot be eaten anywhere else in the world. How does he know? He lives in your city. He knows this street, even though there are so many streets to know. This city is too big to know as well as people in other cities can know their cities, but people do know this city. It is a big and powerful city. It is famous like a movie star. It is a common place to speak about, a popular place, even people who have not been to your city know about your city. Still some people who live in this city are not from here and never will be and they will never know this city like the people of this city know the city. I am trying to tell you that this city is a big city and it has its people and its people know who they are and what can be found on their streets.

There is a woman who traveled to the man's city.

Your city is so big. There are so many people in it. There are so many things happening at one time. I know somewhere in this city there is a sign, above a store, at a station, on cardboard or paper, being written by a child or a homeless man somewhere with something I would want to say to you.

The Priests of the City Bless their People on the Trains.

Hey, folks. Listen up. I'm homeless. I live on the streets. There are evil things on these streets. I've seen them. There are evil things on the streets. If anybody cares you can give me a dollar. Again, folks. I'm homeless. If anybody cares you can contribute a dollar.

God bless you.

God bless you.

God bless you.

The woman travels to the man's city.

I miss you. It is so beautiful and ugly here. I stop. I stop on the street while the people move around me. I tilt my head to the side and that row of buildings flatten to become paintings of different genres displayed on a wall. Buildings in shades of green and baby blue, thin buildings and thick buildings. Buildings who say I am soft and pretty. Buildings who speak all the time. Decorated buildings and plain buildings. The horizon becomes the skyline. Which one did you say was your favorite? This sideline vision. This whole city feels like a busy bar. People are walking towards and away from each other struggling to get to their drinks, their destination. People are comfortable brushing up against my shoulders and chest and grasping my arms to get to their destination. I am so close to the people of your city. I can smell the sweat and perfume and drinks on their bodies. If I stretch my chest out and walk towards them bravely they will have to touch their chests to my chest. If I brush up against them intentionally, pretending I don't know the dance of the city, I can pretend you are with me. You come alone, and you sit down, and you don't know who you will meet here. This whole city feels like a busy plane going everywhere. You don't know who will speak what language when or how. You will sit next to someone and you don't know who they will be, or who they will become. Maybe it will turn out to be someone you would have chosen to sit next to, if you could choose in the city.

The woman who missed the man and then traveled to his city travels to another city to forget about him.

This other city is even bigger than your city. I have come here to forget you. It feels more dangerous than your city because there are so many more people here, but it is a safer city. Everybody looks the same here. They all have the same hair color, and the same eye color, and there are only a few shades of skin color that this city's people share. There are large brown buildings in this city, but they are all the same. It is so obvious here that concrete is made of sand. These buildings look like buildings made out of sand by the hands of children. They carry stains of dirt and grime just like a face. There are so many cars in this city. They are not moving. The cars cannot move there are too many. But the people are moving right next to the cars. All the people are yelling at each other from inside and outside the cars. The people walking are yelling at the people driving. And all the cars are honking. The cars are sharks and the people are fish, the people are sharks and the cars are fish. The smoke of the cars makes my face dirty constantly. The people put their bodies up against the cars so they can keep moving. They are as slick as the dirty starved cats who live here. They live in the corners where the garbage is dumped by the people. There are dirty starved dogs here too. They sleep on top of cars and howl all night long like wolves. This is a city that makes you feel if you threw a piece of bread, or your shirt, out a window somebody would take it. Somebody would need it. This is a dirty city where nothing is wasted. This is a city who does not waste. How can a womb not be poisoned in this place? On the streets animals are trapped in cages so small they cannot move. The people have no sympathy, they are trapped in small places too. This is the strength their city teaches them. That is the beauty of this city, here people cannot feel sympathy for an animal. I have seen here sea creatures with their fins up against glass and mammals who cannot move their tails. The way you said let's do this, as you touched my head gently. Every time I think about this I will shiver, something electric will travel down from my heart down to my gut down to my crotch. A pleasant sensation. The stench in these markets. How could their food still taste good when it comes from a place that smells so bad? But it does taste good. It tastes better than the food in our cities. Flies and stray dirty starved cats are everywhere in this market. Cats prowl on little hills made of years of the slime from decay and grime under their filthy paws and my feet. You realize it was all once slime that turned into something. The story of the city. Everything was just something black you walk on. And the flies want to land on anything they can land on. They can land anywhere and be happy at this market. The flies look like they may be the only happy things in this city, the only creatures that have what they need. Dirty beach umbrellas keep the sun away from the food and the people. This slime is what life was made of years and years ago. Under my feet, this is what life was before the city. Something dies and rots and becomes this black stuff under my feet. Cats and flies and food and dirt and people reaching for money and food while standing very close to each other. There is so much noise in the market. Sound becomes an object, like the food under the umbrellas, like the slime on the ground that has made little black hills under the feet of the people. The people's words can be heard individually, or heard together. Noticing the difference between words here is similar to noticing the difference between the fly on my eyelid and the flies that dot everything, concentration. The market smells like decay but the streets smell like rotten fruit. The people in this city love perfume shops and some of them also need to shit on its streets. The smell of these corners and trash and perfume together becomes the smell of fruit dying. The city is breathing.

The woman having traveled to his city and another city goes back to her own city.

All cities look the same in pictures. Me standing next to a building. Me standing next to cars and signs. I am back in my own city. I have not forgotten you. I am not like that homeless man. I am better than the homeless. You said look at your pussy. It's so beautiful. Look at this, your lips and your clit. Are your lips sensitive? How does this feel? Then you put your mouth on me. Your pussy is tight and warm. I was hard all night. Of course, I wanted you. Of course I want you. But I can't make love to you right before you take off to a different city. Of course I. Want you. Of. Course I want. You. Why doesn't he want me? Jesus is coming? Are you ready? Why? I am not like the homeless. I will not be crazy like the homeless people. Some people have to be alone their whole lives. I will not be crazy like the homeless. I will have another person love me. My pussy is beautiful. My pussy is beautiful. Jesus, help me not be so sad. I am not like these people waiting for buses, Jesus. Why don't I want to live right now? I wanted to live when he wanted me, but now I don't. It's because he wanted to touch my body and this made my body happy, so it made it all right to have a body. If I were in danger I would also want to live. Danger makes me want to save my body. Love and danger are what make us want to live. Love and danger are distractions. Nothing makes sense. Nothing in the city makes sense now.

We were going to go to an Indian restaurant and have tea at that fancy hotel and go to the best seafood restaurant in the city and the best Italian restaurant in the city. In your city we went to an Indian restaurant and a park where they were shooting a commercial and then we went for tea at a place that is famous for its teas. Then we went to a music hall where we didn't like the music and then we went to an Irish bar. Then we were in his bed and he put his arms around me and he stroked my hips back and forth with one finger. And then he put his hands on my face and turned it towards his face slowly and put his lips on mine. When do you want to make love? Who do you want to make love? Why do you want to make love? Where do you want to make love? What do you want to make love? How do you want me to make love to you? How will you want me to? The homeless go crazy and can go without love. They can live without making love. They don't walk around this city with this gnawing inside them for him. Nothing gnaws at the homeless. They want different things and they can have those things by begging. What if I don't deserve any more love than the homeless do?

What if I don't deserve love?

What if you deserve love but people don't always get what they deserve?

Bad people get away with things because people don't always get what they deserve.

Good people don't have things they want because people don't always get what they deserve.

The woman comes back to her own city.

I am back in my city. I must have come here to fall in love. Cities are made by their people. Cities make their people. But I must have come to this city so it can make me. I thought it would be where I would find love. Maybe I wanted to have a house and a man and children. Maybe I wanted to grow old alone in a house and die. Maybe I wanted my children to come stare at me alone in my bed before I died and an old man to be by my side. Now I walk with my arms outstretched towards the tall buildings in front of me as if I could keep walking until I have all those buildings in my arms. My arms are wrapped around those buildings and I am in the buildings' chests being held back by the buildings. The bosoms of buildings. This is how the city is holding me. The smoke of these cars, it is the city's breath in my face. And as I keep walking I make little noises, soft sounds, leave my mouth unintentionally. Yesterday, I looked out at the city from where I was sitting in a coffee shop. The signs on the buildings and the trees in between the buildings are changing colors. The city felt multicolored. I wanted to stop feeling this sadness so I could enjoy the day. A beautiful day in a beautiful city. When it occurred to me as I tried to imagine, or will, happiness. I understood. What had I ever felt before, without this sadness? I had felt nothing. I could not see the colors because they were only color. They were not the details of the beautiful day I have to see that I cannot see. Before this sadness there was nothing. Suddenly, there were tables and glasses and plates and chairs and signs and waiting for him to come touch me. I remember I could see color without it being smeared by this black cloud of sadness. But it was only color. I will let the sorrow live in my chest and feel it rather than wanting it gone. I will let it spread tentacles, branches so it becomes a tree like creature inside a fence, so that it becomes a part of this city. It started as a dark flower. It started as a blossom bursting with seeds of black liquid. I became something like other things in the city. Then it reached for me. Now I want to touch people only when they are far away, but I am alone without the noise they make when they are close. I want them to stay away from me only when I am surrounded by them. In a busy street I feel alone. When I am alone I feel as if they are all suffocating me. I hear the lady say to her dog no, Leah. Stop, Puppy. I'm sorry. Did she scare you? She asks me a question. I want to kiss the lady. So I don't look at the lady. I want to be the puppy, Leah. I want. I want now. I can want because of you. I have this, and the city.

THE PEOPLE SPEAK

Why do the people of the city speak to me? They don't realize the consequences. There are people here willing to kill you. The people of this city would be willing to kill me. Now I know this. There is only a thread of order holding the city together, keeping these people from killing each other, from killing me. The people of this city would eat me alive, they would eat flesh off of my body while I writhed. I must be on the lookout. I must remember to never forget this. The only reason they are not beating me . . . there is the thin thread, a thin thread. There is much more evil in this city than there is good. Most people would kill me to survive. Most people are bad. That is why it is only sad when children die, because you can't know yet if they have chosen to be bad like most people or if they had decided to be good. If you kill ten children you are killing only one good person but you don't know which one of them it is yet. And at any time you can experience a random act of unkindness. Random acts of unkindness performed by the angry people. I go get a cup of coffee and the woman handing it to me could spill it on me intentionally or throw it in my face, if she wanted. A person behind me could grab my body or take something I need to live from my pockets. Anybody could yell at me at any minute. These people are cannibals in the jungle. They are only calm momentarily after they have had an outlet for their rage. They will be good only when they are supposed to be good and kill when they are supposed to kill. They can wait and wait, then they may kill and eat. This is what they do here. They are good to each other then they kill each other. There are no tribes here. They are bad to each other so they can be good to each other. I live in a big city. Nobody will eat me. Nobody will eat me. I will not let them eat me.

AFTER THAT MAN DID THAT TO HER

She cried all the way from his store to the other store. She told the people at the other store who asked her if she was all right that she was sick. And on her way back home she thought about how cold it is and how the homeless will die tonight. What good is it to live in a city if nature too can still kill you? She cried when she got home. She paced around with her arms flailing. Then she walked to her locked door and kissed it gently. She pressed her lips to the door over and over slowly with her mouth slightly open because she was safe because the door was locked. Her lips moved against it as if that patch of door was the forehead of a person who had saved her. They can't take her door away from her. Not today because she paid this month to have this door. She thought about writing cruel things on his door. This cruel man is a stupid fucking Korean. This Korean man is cruel. Or maybe it would hurt him more if she wrote this Korean man is good. It will make him feel guilty. Maybe it would make him think about what he did to her. Why do I want him to regret what he did to me? I don't know him. I don't know him? This is just how he is. He is angry. He won't regret what he did to me ever because he thinks I am stupid. He thinks I am the one who is stupid. He is cruel and cruel people don't regret being cruel because that is what they have chosen. Why do I want the stranger to regret what he did to me? He might not even have been trying to be cruel to me. But he might have been. How would I know why he did what he did? He is a stranger. Why did he do that to me? He doesn't even know me. What's the point of being so angry with a stranger? I could try making myself feel better by thinking about how I have a better life than he does and pretend he acted that way because his life is harder than mine. But that probably isn't true. I could think about how I am a better person but that doesn't make me feel better. What keeps any of them from all jumping out from behind their counters and coming to get me? What holds this city together? Who tells the people what to do? He has to be nice to me because I am a customer. He didn't even want my money. How could he have not wanted to be nice to me, for my money? How could he not have wanted my money? What do I want him to feel? I want him to feel guilty for what he did to me. I want him to know I didn't do anything to him. But if he was capable of feeling guilt then he wouldn't have done that to me. He must be one of the people in this city who would split me open with an ax if he had the chance, or if he needed to. If what was holding this city together fell apart. He was talking to a stranger. Why? Why would you talk like that to a stranger? That was just a random act of unkindness. Random act of unkindness. People always want to fight me here. They think I am trying to get on the bus for free, trying to dirty the bus with my feet, trying to steal. They will stop you and yell at you whenever they want. They think you are trying to get away without a pass. They will make you go back and get one even if they have seen your pass before. They think you are trying to not pay for your food. They always get to decide. You won't let people talk to you that way anymore. So many strangers. So many people if you let them talk to you a certain way you will never be done with it. What do the people want from you? They decide how they will talk to others. Teach them how to talk to you. Some people they see, but not you. What do they want? They don't see what you want. You are in the way of what they want. You are in my way. Move, move, move that's all you are. Watch where you put that. Get out of my store. We don't have that here. Watch where you're going. Keep moving. Where are you going? That's all you are to them.

It is better to withdraw amongst many than to be alone.
It is better to withdraw amongst many than to be alone.
It is better to withdraw amongst many than to be alone.
It is better to withdraw amongst many than to be alone.
It is better to withdraw amongst many than to be alone.
It is better to withdraw amongst many than to be alone.
It is better to withdraw amongst many than to be alone.
It is better to withdraw amongst many than to be alone.
It is better to withdraw amongst many than to be alone.
It is better to withdraw amongst many than to be alone.
It is better to withdraw amongst many than to be alone.
It is better to withdraw amongst many than to be alone.
It is better to withdraw amongst many than to be alone.
It is better to withdraw amongst many than to be alone.
It is better to withdraw amongst many than to be alone.
It is better to withdraw amongst many than to be alone.
It is better to withdraw amongst many than to be alone.
It is better to withdraw amongst many than to be alone.
It is better to withdraw amongst many than to be alone.
It is better to withdraw amongst many than to be alone.
It is better to withdraw amongst many than to be alone.
It is better to withdraw amongst many than to be alone.
It is better to withdraw amongst many than to be alone.

THE STORY OF THE CITY

There are trillions of suns shining at the same time. But we are far away from even our own sun. What does that mean? Four and a half billion years ago the earth was formed. The meteorites are as old as we are so now we have radioactive dating. Bacteria helped create oxygen. Earth. English word, believed to be derived from a Greek word meaning ground. Nicknamed the blue planet because of how it looks from space. Earth is a relatively safe destination if you are from another planet. A massive but short lived star exploded as a supernova. The blast formed the cloud that formed the earth's sun. The ice particles and dust stuck together. They became boulders. Gravity held them together. Asteroids impacted the earth and created tremendous heat. The outer rock produced a molten ocean. The first forty million years the iron core generated a magnetic field. It preserves our air. The rocky mantle melted forming volcanoes. Then an impact fused the two layers of earth together. The molten debris from the collision coalesced to shape the moon. We did not see this happen but we know it did because the moon is here. The moon held the tilt steady and this created the seasons. Almost four billion years ago the collisions subsided. When the earth cooled, liquid covered its surface. The origins of water. Where did earth get all its water? Steam from volcanoes became rain, which is old water. Or, new water came from space. Comets crashed into earth to bring it water. They may have also given us bacteria. We did not see this, but bacteria must have come from somewhere in space because it is here. And comets are in space so they must have brought the bacteria. We cannot see gods but something must make mothers want their babies to come back from the dead. Almost four billion years ago there was no oxygen. Or atmospheric chemicals formed a primordial soup that had amino acids, the building blocks of life. Primitive carbon compounds. But single cell organisms lived in oceans. Microbes who can live through the heat in sulfur. Three billion years ago primitive life soaked up energy from the sun. They soaked up light. They made food. They became algae. The algae made oxygen. We have so much in common with bacteria. We owe our lives to the scum of the earth. Four billion years ago heat and pressure produced rock lighter than the ocean floor which floated and created continents. Most of earth's existence was without humans however. We are two seconds out of four billion years. Five hundred million years ago from now the sun will be so hot that people will not exist. So, the things God made are lava to make earth and water to make waves and mountains

God also must have made from the lava. So, water divided into parts who would become lakes, rivers, ponds, and streams. And mountains divided into parts who would become hills, valleys, cliffs made of rocks, and fields. So the things God made are earth and water and sky, which divided into parts like clouds and stars and sun and moons. The things people made were made out of the things God made. They are buildings which are made of stone and plastic and steel and wood from trees, sand to make glass and concrete. The bags and carts and tires and books in the city are all made by people from things God made first. What else were the people suppose to do but make things out of other things? The people made fake stars and fake trees and fake sky after God made the real sky and trees and stars. And now the city . . . The people first made the city when the people needed to live by the water so they could eat the fish. They all started to live close to each other instead of traveling so far apart. They had to keep the things they made out of the things God made together so they built places where they could sleep and keep things. So, they needed places to sell things since they could keep all their things in one place, and now could need more things. That is why the city is full of places to buy things and places to sleep. And since the people weren't moving around anymore, and it was easy to buy things, they had to find other ways to keep busy.

A MAN SAYS SMILING

At a park they are sitting on grass. He motions to her smiling, come here. Reaches out with both his arms then pulls them both back towards his body, come here. Sit by me, he motions to her smiling so she can sit by him, not across from him. She cringes on grass. Make yourself comfortable, he says. Spread out on the grass if you want. Later he puts his hands on top of hers sitting next to her in a car. She cringes in a car. What else is it? Earlier he saw her twice. He has seen her twice already, once sitting on a step outside a restaurant, then once again standing on a street outside her apartment. Unintentionally both times, both times didn't have to happen, but they did. They did happen. He has sat on a bus where a woman was laughed at by men for smelling like garlic, and she was laughed at even more when she sprayed herself with cheap perfume on the bus, and yelled at because of the smell of her perfume until she started to mumble and cry. He has sat on a bus where an old man whose mind was like a child's repeated I like you, I like you, while smiling at a young woman who laughed at him. He has sat on a busy bus where a man tried to give his seat up for a woman who refused to sit where he sat. You'll find someone, she says. I found you, he says smiling. Then he says, it's too late I already found you, in a panic. Don't you see what I see, a man smiling at you, reaching for you, wanting to put his hands on yours? What else is it?

THE PEOPLE SPEAK

Why do the people in this city speak to me? Every time, every time they speak. They take the risk of hurting someone by just speaking like themselves. You can make someone sad when you speak to them, you know? Like me when I used to be bad, but now I'm good. When I used to do bad things, now I'm good and do good things. I used to not understand the bad people, but now I do because I used to be bad. They are everywhere on the street. They try to touch me so I have to move away and keep walking. Every time you see one you have to move away. I think everybody is stealing from me but I will never forget when they did once. I said once she is stealing from you, once when really I was stealing from her, trying to hide it by thinking she is stealing from me. I still remember that. She was yelling at me, I remember a long time ago, that is when it happened that way, and when I said I felt bad over and over again and she yelled at me. I was young then so I have to be nice to young people because they don't know anything either, even if they do they may think or do something that is wrong. But it may change and be right again someday. It may change, why it mattered. You don't know if they're good or bad the little children so you can't hurt them. You don't kill the babies because we don't know if they're good or bad yet. Which ones will be good and which ones will be bad? We don't know. I used to be bad now I'm good because I'm nice to children.

Killer

It is romantic when she and she dine with oak and candles and cloth

she is the willow of the streets

her hair falls down her back like it wants to keep from falling

silk and water

she would hold his head up with her bare hands her palms flat against sweat and pores

he is hungry he wants to eat and drink and see and sleep

her hair floats against the sky

wings and water

she is the lighthouse in the middle of the street

men speak in different tongues with flicks and sparks

and she and she and she and we the hair that grows out the wells makes its way attaching writhing with limbs

he wants to eat and move and see with arms and legs and face

he wants to look at all the different shapes and figures and colors

look out the glass and want an apple or blue paint

the bitterness takes him

makes him say things he wants to say

now it is a hat or a boat in front of his feet

to think the brick of the walls is so beautiful and not know why

a baby wants shapes and figures and colors

what would it have been like to have been loved

having an outside organ to touch and feel or know when it needs to be cleaned

skin and water

what color would it be and what shape

having an ice pick in your chest

removed

to have been loved by a mother might have felt like the body belonged to the sea

without the fear

to have been loved by a father

to receive a gift that is not a reminder that it is not you who receives gifts

why is everything more beautiful while it is swaying in the wind

her hair is a wispy finely shredded straw

People

Slowly lips part and a kiss is blown by the man whose spit is still on your face. It is a fact that things feel good and then feel bad. When you lose a child who is still inside you bleed from down the middle, but once the child is outside you do not bleed unless you cut yourself. You feel like your flesh is made of paper you feel like a small paper boat in the middle of the still black ocean. There is no horizon in sight. Man can pave streets and lights and control the trees with black ornate poles and sharp edged prism prisons. Lest the trees desire to run . . . blocks of copper and teal and maroon tiles and the stars are above. But how do you change how you feel? If an asteroid hits earth we will all die, but still the mother sits by her child when she knows she wants to die. People are so lonely, all 12 billion of them. It is true that humanity will be the end of the earth. The earth would be safer without us. If we had never been there . . . what does a small baby want to be before it dies? Without us which of the creatures would know that they were happy, because they had once been so sad. One bad day makes the next one good. First you cannot see or you do not know, and then you can. You are alone, then when you are not...there is no cup or bowl . . . but then you can find one. If the earth died we would be sad, then happy. If all color disappeared . . . then we would be happy with shades of brown. Why do we stop the old when we find the new? Here are some things the people don't like . . . physical suffering. Like from cold or torture or disease. They don't like it when nobody loves them or when people they love die. They like to accomplish things. Speak in accents and dance. Then they go to new places to see new things. Until feeling good does not feel good. What do you want?

To make people do what you want them to do. And say what you want them to say. No, you have to love people even when they don't want the same things or even when they say things that hurt you. And do things to make you feel bad. But if they don't' choose, you are not happy with what they say that does not hurt you. When a woman is powerful she is more powerful than a man. The large women who men want to be large feel full of everything on the outside like they could be on the inside. The small women who men want to be small feel that they are not carrying heavy loads on their bones.

If a demon hand reached for me sleeping in the night, I would not be afraid. I would take the opportunity to put my face against it and beg to know the nature of god.

How do the birds survive flying in such filthy air?

But when they come home even if it's for an hour, and there is nothing to do, what do they do?

She did not tell them about the knives, but about being called an owl.

Murder would be meaner if even the murderer was not going to die too. If you took life something that otherwise somebody could keep, if when you took life you were taking something someone could actually keep.

The veins of the body looks so much like roots of trees.

The corpse of the whale the sea absorbs, but too much oil from the corpses under the earth . . . What each person sees when they say freedom makes it impossible for all of them to fight for the same thing.

I just wanted to be from some beautiful city.

Why is the city beautiful?

The buildings are like canyons that can be traversed. They are not just shells for the fragile bodies of the people, they are giants with spines made by the people. The people walk in and in between them. The glass buildings are like frozen waves or rectangular icicles. The people walk amongst the buildings. They cross each other and brush up against each other in a dance they know. That is why the people of this city cannot be known by their skin color, but rather by their movements. Though nothing surprises the people of the city. Men and women may make music for the people in between the buildings. There are trees and lights and buildings in a frozen dance with each other. And at night when the people get in their cars they can see that the cars on the freeways and highways make up lights that make the tiers of roads look like those of the cosmos. The lampposts are like guardians, arms holding up a light, and there are so many. In the taxis there are people waiting to take you places, and on the streets the people in carts are waiting to feed you. And all of the city's structures make a line that reaches up and out and down turning the sky into only a frame.

There are all kinds of people in the city.

Do not thank him for that fucking quarter.

Don't thank them for giving you some fucking change.

You're just asking for some change.

They will think that you think that you don't deserve it.

They will think you think you don't deserve it.

They will think you think you don't deserve it.

Thank them when they give you something they would give another human being.

As long as there are so many people around you
you will not crave to be around any people.

As long as there are so many people around
you you should not crave to be around any people.

As long as there are so many
people around you you will not crave to be around any people.

As long as there are so many people around you you will not crave
to be around any people.

As long as there are so many people around you you will not crave
to be around any people.

As long as there are so many people around you you will not crave
to be around any people.

There are many kinds of people in the city.

A man says I see you, Ms. Pretty. Then he does a dance for you when you pass by again and he says you got yourself an ass, baby.

A woman says you look like you believe in people power. Yes, you can be a member. Come on, give me a hug. You can give me a hug right now.

A mime with a face painted white holds a sign that says "come talk to me" as a woman next to him tells you it's worth it, believe me, I didn't want to stop for him either . . . it's worth the time.

A woman says buy this. Support the homeless.

And this man always plays the flute with a sign that says "will give lessons", and as he plays he dances closer and closer to you, every time you pass by.

Hi, baby. Hey, baby.

Thank you for supporting . . .

                                                    white man white coat sitting down

                            bald brown man black glasses reading blue book

                                                                                 white man white coat

                              white old man brown coat reading big black book

                                                                                    white man white coat

                                                                                       white man white coat

                                                                                       white man white coat

             white man white glasses blue coat looking out window while holding on to rail

black man black hat black coat reading brown book standing up

brown woman brown coat brown gloves writing something down in a book

white woman pink hair gray sweater blue eyes standing holding on to rail

                                                                                   white man white coat

white man white coat

white man white coat

white man white coat

white man white coat

white man white coat

Why is the city beautiful?

If you could stare down from above, in the mornings, the city would look like an atom with many parts moving away from and coming back to each other, circling each other while moving towards each other. If you could stare down from above the city, at night, the city would look like a starry sky, the still darkness shattered by scattered light.

Why is the city beautiful?

There are days in this city when you notice that the hard ground is paved to smooth your way as trees lining the street act like canopies made of slender fingers, an arm a hand and millions of fingers, the sun hits buildings so that half of everything is of a yellow hue, a transparent gold, and people are making food for you in small movable spaces and people are waiting to take care of you and waiting to take you places, and even more people are waiting for you to cross the street so they can walk next to you in many different colors of clothes and skin of different colors and you still feel you are in a moving painting when you walk onto the train and they are waiting to sit next to you, waiting to protect you from whatever will happen to all of you together.

Why is the city beautiful?

The city has tamed the water and trees.

The trees are chained in the city and the water is contained.

Remember, when the city is young buildings can be quickly ripped down and built back up because this speaks of progress.

When the city is old every building removed creates a small rip, a scar for the people who know what has been replaced when they look. Where the city is stretched its skin breaks and leaves marks.

The poet said that love is a hut with water and a crust and so is the city.

Your feet could only take you so far here.

It is like a planet with a horizon you cannot manage alone.

The city tames nature and puts trees on the roofs of multicolored buildings.

Buildings garnished with all the colors of fragile flowers.

Why is the city beautiful?

The people of the city can see a homeless man next to his homeless dog and feel pity for the dog and not the man. This alone is something beautiful. They are not afraid of the homeless, or the crazy people who say things about the world ending on street corners, or the people who make music or food for them. Not anymore. They are accustomed to these things. They are proud to be from the city. You see, civilization is the city, which is made of their waste. But if your city is big enough, nothing will go wasted. Somebody will be willing to pick at your garbage. Somebody will be willing to eat your garbage, somebody will sleep in your garbage tonight.

A DATE IN THE CITY

Let's drink this cup of coffee outside on the street. Yes, it is an outdoor café. This will help us feel in love, sitting here across from the caged trees and the beautiful buildings. These things make the streets beautiful, an outdoor café on a beautiful street. The cars pass by, their noise combines in with our words making them more important. Buildings tower over us, over the trees. It's hard to meet single women here you know? You don't know who's single here because there are so many people in this city you can't know them all or know which ones to speak to. This is such a big city you can't meet people so easily. Let's walk down the street passing restaurants and diners and café and places that sell things like cameras, and glasses, and furniture, and candy. Do you want to go to the museum? Parking lots with bags of cans and homeless men looking for more cans. I give them money sometimes as an act of random kindness. In this city an act of random kindness can create change. Or an act of random unkindness. At least we are anonymous here. Anonymous. We should go to the hotel, that one that has the bar on the roof where you can see the whole city? Be above the buildings, or chase the pigeons away from a patch of beautiful cobblestone or marble. Look at the old buildings. Everything good fails, that is the glory of the old city. There are still some things in this world made by hand, those are the buildings. There are theaters here from a long time ago that are decorated in their themes so the walls are etched and there are chandeliers. It is amazing that somebody made this building. Will the people of the new city still make things with their hands? What would they think of our city now? Will they think we have made something beautiful? Welcome to this city, where love comes to die, you're so funny. Let's go get something to eat. Where? Anywhere. There are so many places to eat on this street. I take pictures of lost things. There is only ever one shoe on these streets, one bottle, some coins, and pieces of paper with lists sometimes. I have never been to this restaurant before. I have never actually been here before. Cars pass by as we eat outdoors, again. Buy me an ice cream cone and let's walk around the city some more. Stand outside the tree cage outside the place that makes keys and smoke together. Let's walk to the water. This city is built by the water, most cities are. They needed to be built by the water because the people needed to trade because they needed to eat. Now there is very little food for them in these oceans because the city makes everything dirty. They are good to look at and build around though. The water makes more people come and buy things too. The fountains outside these buildings are like the waterfalls of great civilizations. How does a ladybug live here? How can it breathe this air and live? Make a wish. If it stays alive when you blow it away it will come true. If it does not die here in this city? There is a man who puts postcards everywhere, did you hear about him? Yes, and a woman who leaves flowers here in random places. Wow. Restaurants, stores, and hotels. The jagged lines that make the skyline make a thread twisted and gnarled yet symmetrical somehow. Squares and ovals and triangles and rectangles and lines make up the shape of the city. And when the lights come on, above the city and below the city, it is . . . The city is where the trains are and where the homeless people try to sleep. It is warmer underground. An old man gives a woman who is crying a flower that was bought in a store. Don't leave me yet. Let me take you out, anywhere you want to go. Anywhere in this city? It would make me happy, it would make me feel like a man again. All right. There is this place I have always wanted to go. Good, I love Italian. The lights. The big city sleeps with small lights on, like a young child. A restaurant that has real Italian people and it looks like an Italian restaurant on the inside. No, wait. Don't walk alone in this city. It is nighttime. It is dangerous. At night the people in this city can kill or rape you or take your things. In the mornings the people in this city can take your things too but the light of the sun keeps them from killing you. Let me walk you home there are less cars down this street. But there are lights on all the trees. Everything we need is here. Phones, and books, and clothes and candy. If we take this street and that street we can get somewhere sooner. No, trust me I have memorized some of these streets. The ones that I have been on in this city. I will drive you anywhere when I have a car. Actually, I am going to have a little baby. I will keep it even though I don't have to in this city. Traffic generation, the more highways you build the more traffic there will be. I will go live in the country with my mother then. Does your mother love you? Look at these lights like lightning bugs. We are all insects attracted to lights. No, we are just people, we need the lights or we can't see. Stay here. You can be anything here. The best of anything you are going to be. Nobody will know you because there are so many people here. Nobody can know who is the best at something in this city because there are way too many people. Lightning bugs around a tree and lights around a tree. We are all like those moles or mice or bears in cartoons who have tree houses in forests. We have to put these trees in cages so we can put the lights on them so this city can be beautiful. Shit, this traffic! We could be in that traffic. We are all hanging on by a thread. You can park cars on the road though. Yes, you can walk in and out of cars. Life in the cars and on the buses and on the trains is all the same. Yes! From above the lights of the city right before dawn, they are like stars in black, starry space. Only in a city would people ever need superheroes, you know? You have to have superpowers to fly over these buildings and lift these cars. You need them to move mountains too. But here you need the superpowers just to save all the people.

Tonight, right now, if your city is big enough, then right now, there and two young men and one young woman beating up one homeless woman on one of its streets. If your city is big enough then they kicked her one last time before they ran away. If your city is big enough then a man is saying to another man right now that he will call the police. If your city is big enough then right now there is a man in a car driving slowly past a girl. If your city is really really really big then there is an injured bird that a woman has placed in box and two boys are kicking that box and laughing while the bird startles. There is a drunk woman right now in bed with her two little boys. And a man and a woman and two boys are eating ice cream in a car. If you live in a very big city then there are two girls now throwing a boy's shoes on the roof because they hate him because he is ugly. A man somewhere in your city is being beaten with sticks by another man. A girl in a car sees this and tells her mother to keep driving. But this is only true if your city is big enough.

Of course, I'm afraid of the homeless people. I don't have any money to give them. I do say no sometimes but they keep asking and they will keep asking and asking. I am afraid that one of these days I will say sorry, I don't have anything to give you then one of them will say that's all right just show me your titties and I'll try to get away but he will follow me I won't be able to go and he'll grab my breasts and push me around while groping me and by the time anybody sees us it will be too late because he will have touched me everywhere already. One of them saw me take out a dollar for her from a pocket that had twenties. She said you got those big twenties there give me one of those I don't get paid. I just kept thinking about how she could kill me. I thought she would follow me, but she didn't. Anybody could have a twenty, maybe she will go kill somebody else, but she knows I have a twenty. She is sure of it. I showed her. Why did I do that? Never show them your money again. Never carry more than a dollar in that pocket. Please, I need to get me a place and something to eat she said. One of them wanted me to give him money because he was playing the flute. Girl, I need to make my sales. I have too much money in my pocket. They can come after you if they are already sure you have it there waiting for them. They can come get you. Once when I missed the train and had to walk home early in the morning I had to give two of them twenties. They asked for a dollar and I was scared. They said they needed a hotel room and that their daughter had asthma and she was waiting for them in the old hotel room. When I pulled out the dollar they saw my twenties. Can we give you back the dollar and get those twenties? I gave it to them so they don't kill me. They can follow you. But, after spring and summer and fall then there is winter. They are quiet in the winter because they are so cold.

The city is made of sand. The cement needed for its buildings, the glass embedded in its buildings, and the concrete that is its ground are all made of sand. The beautiful stained glass of its cathedrals is only sand. All cities then are desert cities. All cities then come from the sea.

Can you smell the perfume that leaves its shops and the shit from its street corners? They do come together to make the city smell of dead fruit. Can you understand why? Can you imagine how sweet and rotted the breath of this city can be?

To whom in this city am I more than just a story?

An orange has skin imprinted with many tiny holes like pores. The skin of an orange is only always the color of what's inside it. The orange's body is calved. The body of an orange is split yet joined and protected. Inside the orange is a family of slender crescent moons cocooning inside skin of a similar color.

Who in this city would cry if I died?

I know why they gave the heart its shape, a circular target with wings and a tail can be easily spotted and stabbed. It is where I want to be stabbed. I know why they say pain comes from this organ, the heart. It is where in my chest I need to be stabbed. I turned suddenly and felt a pinch near where the knife and kettle lay on the counter. I thought the knife had entered my stomach and was relieved for an instant. A sensation started from my crotch up to my gut up to my chest. But it was only the edge of the counter that had pressed into me. I feel it now. Everybody in this world is all alone. Every body is its own planet where words circle trying to collide, but can only orbit. All the words people are trying to make are misunderstood. All people work to be loved by other people when what they really want is each other's flesh. I too would raise a child in this big ugly city just so something can sleep against my chest. This city has so many people in it. I see all of them now without their bodies or faces. They are things or spirits or something. There is a woman who is so sad she would look as if she is trying to eat her own mouth if she ever cried. There is a man who just realized there is nothing you can do to make another person love you. You can call or stop calling or say or stop saying but they will never love you. If you are gone they will not long for you. When I see without my eyes my skin burns with ice. I crawl and squawk and squirt words. If I had a real face here in front of me I could be happy. One real face could erase all the faceless people I see. But there is nobody. I won't call anybody anymore. They all think I am crazy. What could I do to make words mean something? If you do what, then you can bring a word back to its meaning? How are you? There is no meaning in that now. I will call somebody. If I die I would be a story. If I stabbed myself in the heart I would be a story people tell about a man who lived in a building who stabbed himself in the heart. I am a crazy man who lived here.

Son, if you attack this man now then you have to stay fierce. At any minute if you let up with it, just a little, well, then you will just be a man holding another man in your arms. If you come at him you have to stay strong, boy, or for one second you will look like you are only trying to hold on to a man, son.

This city is so big, nobody is from here. The bigger the city the higher you will have to lift your head to see the sky. The bigger the city the less scared its people will be of walking next to the cars. The bigger the city the more noise it will make. The bigger the city the more proof of life there is to be found there. Remember, the most evidence that people exist is found in cities. This is why when a whole city is destroyed it is the saddest thing. The bigger the city the more broken glass you will find on its sidewalks.

When you can see the clouds below you and the sun's rays beam through a carpet of clouds to make a spectrum of light and you are in a plane that breaks through the mountain kingdom of clouds you realize that clouds can be one thing enough to have and make a color but still they can't carry you. You cannot walk on them like you can the streets of this city.

If you have never seen the lights of the city as they beam across the water through the trees under the bridge making heavy thick rainbow beams of light like many suns of many colors so thick and heavy like paints melted then you do not know the meaning of the words shimmer or reach or glide then or what it means when people say you are going towards the light.

The sky is so much more beautiful when it is only a frame around the buildings and trees of the city. The city alone is proof that we too can make things larger than ourselves, like mountains and trees, just like God. Yes, it is not only God who makes big things.

The city is an unnatural beauty. But it is natural as well. The buildings are made from the earth and sea. The cement and glass are made from sand. The people make the city like bees make hives. But the city can still be ugly or beautiful in certain lights depending on whether or not it is clean or dirty just like the people who made it.

Because on the trains they all sit alone while surrounded by each other. All these people, they all know how to look and for how long, they know how they may stare for too long and what would happen next, they know how to be here now.

Think of all the shapes that occur in nature. The shape of leaves the shape of a mountain or flowers or stars and jumble them in any order where they are etched in big and small and colored and shaded and stretched and then you can begin to understand what is possible to consider when you are staring at one of these buildings.

The bridges are just like the buildings only opened up from the inside out folded up and down and dug out from the inside.

I no longer enjoy walking down the streets of this city. Even now in the winter when the people walk slowly. The city used to make me happy, when I knew the people with clean coats had a home away from the snow. The snow now covers these buildings with a sheath of white as if I am seeing the city through a fallen milky sky, and I do not feel it. As if clouds have fallen down to the ground, and I do not feel this. My heart must be broken. I no longer remember. I no longer love walking down these beautiful tree lined streets in the snow. I can't feel why I enjoyed the stained glass windows of its cathedrals or the sunsets hiding in between its buildings or crossing its bridges alone.

People in the city are alone in their beds.

This was just like that other time she was tired after work. She went into that empty restaurant, ordered a sandwich, took a bite of that sandwich, then just fell asleep right where the ketchup had been on her plate. She woke up to waiters laughing, with ketchup on her face. What did she do? What did she do? She had to just sit up, close her mouth, wipe the ketchup off, and keep eating.

People in the city are alone in their beds.

He's not going to do it. He is not going to call her. Why is he not going to call her? Why is he not going to call? Because of all the times he was sure he was right, then turned out to be wrong. He has to make sure now that he doesn't want anything until he first knows whether or not he can get what he wants. If it turns out to be something he can get, then he will know that he has wanted it all along. If it is something he can't have, then he will know to have always hated it. He hates her, that ugly, stupid bitch. She is too short, big nosed, dumpy. Short. She is too short.

People in the city are alone in their beds.

All she knows is that if her father were dying she would really take care of him. She would not make him feel what she has felt about herself. She will not make him feel worthless like he made her feel. She will do this because he would be dying, not because he ever did anything for her. Because she knows what death means now. Because when her mother died it made her wonder if it matters, anything that anybody makes anybody else feel.

People in the city are alone in their beds.

What is the difference between a hunger strike and a sleep strike? Those Irish guys didn't eat, and the Indian guy didn't eat, but nobody ever threatens to stop sleeping. It would probably fuck you up just as much, maybe even more. But you would probably fall asleep accidentally, that's why. Still, why don't people try to stop sleeping? At least try. You'd have to have more guts to stop sleeping than to stop eating, I bet. It would mean more in the end. Maybe I am not sleeping in protest of something? I want to sleep. I just fucking wish I could sleep. The planet rolls around. All the people on it get dizzy and slam into each other. It's the world. That's why people fight. It's the friction. We keep bumping and grinding. Bumping. Grinding. The Bump and Grind. The planet spins, so the people on it get dizzy, so they bump into each other. They bump and grind into each other. That's what makes all the love and all the fighting.

PEOPLE IN THE CITY ARE ALONE IN THEIR BEDS

I would rather be in a very expensive hotel room right now. I want to spend every day walking and eating. But I can't ever eat as much as I want to eat. Whenever I do get to eat. I'm distracted by everything. I'm too easily moved. But I'm only happy when I eat. Then there's a reason to keep doing something. There's a reason to keep chewing. If I could eat all day then sleep all night. I don't know how to spend my days. That's the problem. I only ever want to stare at moving objects. While I eat. What else is there to do all day? What do other people do all day and all night? Wake up and get the kids ready to go to school then go to work then come home then make dinner then eat then get the kids ready to sleep. Maybe you have to clean up a little every single day. I don't have kids and I don't have a job. I clean sometimes. I do work sometimes. But even when I do work I come home and just sit. I turn on the television because I want to just stare at something while I eat. I finish eating then I want to smoke and drink. When I can't keep doing this I don't know what else to do. I don't like staring at the television without something in my mouth. It makes me feel like I'm just wasting time. Seashells are so beautiful because the water and sand moves over them until they form symmetrically ragged patterns, but they do not know they are beautiful. I should write a book. A real book. A real big story. Something that has never been done before. The television says if you kill a butterfly, one year later there are a million less people in the world. What if you kill an ant or a beetle? If you kill a rat are there one million more people in the world one year later? I can't think of a story right now. A girl falls down a rabbit hole. A war a man an odyssey. Some people probably just write until they fall asleep. Maybe it will just come to me. I will hate the writing when it does. I hate the moving of the hands and the making of the mistakes. Errors. Mistakes. You make the mistakes. Then you have to fix the mistakes. Only more proof that everywhere you go. Everything you do. You are just making mistakes and trying to erase mistakes. If I could write all day though. Then I would have something to do. Then I could sleep all night without feeling as if I've wasted all that time. All day. I would be so tired then. I would just fall asleep. I want to want to know about things without having a reason to know them. While I am smoking I am happy because I put the cigarette in my mouth and I have something to do because there is something to take in until it is finished so I only think about that. I used to believe that being stabbed would be the most horrible pain because it would be the pain of a cut multiplied by thousands but then I heard a woman on television say that she didn't feel anything while she was being repeatedly stabbed by her husband but only after when it was all over. This man once told me that he was happy to be retired because he gets to read about all kinds of things he never got to read about before. I wish I could enjoy reading about things and enjoy knowing things. I get so restless. I don't know what to do with myself. I know I have to do something. But what to do? Why should we learn anyway? What good does it do? We learn how to live. What there is in life and how it works. Then we die. Who is fattening this calf for the slaughter? What good is it to let your head become a fat tender calf only to die? Without children or work most of the time. It's hard to fill time. It will be harder to fill time as I get older too. I will be able to do less. And so move less. They say that there is a mind body and spirit connection. I just cannot feel loved and so can't be happy. I tried to but whoever said they loved me. I could not feel it. All three have to be working together for other things to work. Mind. Body. Spirit. The problem is probably with my mind. Or maybe. Probably with my spirit which is affecting my mind which is affecting my body. I wish I could just choose when I died. I don't know what to do. I just don't know. I wish I had a pill. Or a button I could press. So I could choose when to die. If I did I wouldn't worry so much about how much worse things are going to get when I'm older. Then my spirit would be fine and my mind would get better then my body could do things. As it is things could get worse and I would just have to stay here. What do I really need? If there is so little real biological difference between humans and chimpanzees then there is probably no difference at all between people's stories. You can have things in life. People can have other people. They need a place to live. They can make babies who can die but at least give you something to feel while mourning. They can make books. They can make love to their wives and go to work. I do not make love. That wouldn't take up a lot of the time anyway. People used to live in caves. People needed a cave to go back to after they had found food. Sleep is good because while you are sleeping you only have to sleep. You woke up and the day was wasted but now there is nothing else you can do but sleep. You learn how to get to the cave. Which cave is your cave? Then you feel you will always be able to find it again and again. Eventually you like the cave because it begins to smell like you do. Food and drink and shelter. And what else? To really believe you are never going to die. Not really. Because you will go somewhere else or be something else. To feel important. You have a purpose like a tree. Or water. If I shoot myself in the head I might miss. That's why people go through the mouth. You can stay alive if you try to go through the side of the head. Why did people make so many things? You have no idea how many things people made until you have to walk around this city alone just to buy a bar of soap. If you cut your wrists you have to go up and down but not across. What's great about doing things with somebody is it's never a waste of time because you get to feel like you were doing something for somebody. We watched TV. We took a bath together and then ate some pizza. We ate pizza together in the bath. I ate pizza while I was taking a bath. Alone. Tonight. We ate pizza. I just watched TV. All night. You could live if you go across. People made so many things to make themselves feel they are as real as the weeds that grow up through the cracks in the sidewalks they built. Where do you get a cheap strong drink around here? They want to know things. There are so many places they could go. They have thought of everything. Here you see a big city where shiny clean things can be found pulling up near rubble. A city in the snow. A city in the sand. A city in the mountains. A city made of water and sand and rock and wood. Plastic city. Money makes it so you can do things to stay busy. More things to do. See things. Do things. Eat things that won't fill you up. So you can keep eating and eating. I walk around sometimes touching things in the apartment. The clothes in a closet. The inside of a coat. I touch clothes and furniture. Is anything here broken? Fixing is something to do. I'm making sure they are all right. Not ripped. Not broken. Everything is all right. Here is a shirt. Here is a table. What else do people want? A novel would be real success. One book that could change everything. Once God becomes a concept then you have to have to have to stay busy. You write things. He knew. He knows even as she walks beside him now what he would have to do in the end. I would have to make a sentence better than that thought. Think of better stories than the ones that have been told. The objects the people made can survive outside in the snow but the people cannot. The city can take the rain but the people cannot. If you always have to remind yourself that other people have worse lives . . . If you could choose one other person's life and live it in your head . . . If you always have to remind yourself that it can get worse to feel better now . . . But then they have to die too so it wouldn't really matter. Find the God in your every action. But how in this apartment with only these objects to touch. This shirt is not broken. This table is not broken. This floor is clean. Money helps a lot. It helps people stay busy. It helps them maintain the health of their minds and bodies. Stay busy or you think too much. Have a child. Eat good food. Find a hobby. Something you can do until it is time to sleep. Without enough money you cannot even have a window to stare through. The problem is that eating is the only thing that keeps me happy for a while. But I have to eat cheap food and that fills me up quickly and makes me feel sick. It actually causes pain then. Not pleasure. I like to smoke a lot. But if I smoke too much it starts to feel like a fire in my gut. It causes me pain in my throat. I'm only happy when I'm eating or smoking. I don't know what I want. The sound of a siren. A car crash. A car alarm goes off. Someday something even worse than this. I make lists. I organize things. On the street. Sometimes I walk around back and forth. Back and forth. In the apartment I check on everything. I make sure everything is all right. All the objects are fine here. I like to know that I have a year's supply of everything. I start in the kitchen. Yes. Yes. Yes. Sometimes there are mugs in the sink and dust gets everywhere eventually if I don't clean. I wash the mugs. I sometimes drink things. I smoke. I don't have the money to go everywhere I want. Not everywhere. But even if I did live in a fancy hotel I wouldn't be able to eat all day because I would eventually get full. After I got full the eating would become painful. Then I would have nothing to do. I would have to find a way to spend 24 hours of each day. If I sleep for 8 then there would be 16 left. I could stay in bed for 2 of those 16 hours just thinking. Then there would be 14 left. What to do with 14 hours? I would walk around and eat and drink but that would only take up 6. The other 8 hours I could read. But I can't read when I'm restless. I end up touching the book. Just touching it. The cover is not broken. The pages are not folded. The book is clean. I force myself to touch the book until I can read a word. I will just look. Leaf through pages as if a book is an object. The pages of a rosary. Everything is praying if you are alone enough. I could open and close my refrigerator. There is only ice in the freezer. I could check below the sink to make sure I have enough cleaning supplies to last one year. I do enjoy a certain kind of light made by a certain kind of lampshade. I should buy one more in case this one becomes broken. I don't want to die. I feel dead but with pain. That's the problem. It is horrible to know you are inside a body. I don't know what it's like to have just been born anymore. I will die sooner than I was going to before. Every day this happens. I feel things while I'm eating. Peaceful things. When I'm not eating I don't. Eating gives me a purpose. A reason to keep on until I'm finished chewing. I want to be the kind of person who wants to learn things. But I'm not. I could learn things if there were people here to learn them for. I want to go to heaven if there is one. Knowing things doesn't get you to heaven. You could die knowing everything and it doesn't get you anywhere. I should try to learn something that will help me live. Leaning languages won't do that because you need people to speak to in those languages or you forget them. I have no ambition. I regret too much. The more I know about people the less people I can speak to without knowing the people don't want to speak to me anymore. I don't want to know people. Every day I end up smoking and eating cheap food that is too filling. I used to be able to read but now all I can think while reading is who is saying this? Who is trying to speak through the page? Come out. Come out. Come out. Who are you? Why would this person want to speak to me? Then I remember they don't care about me. They don't even know me. They don't know I'm reading this book. I'm touching your book. I wish I could think of a story.

EPISODES

The landlord said that it was only a squirrel. A squirrel who used the attic for shelter at night, so it didn't have to live only in trees, like other squirrels. She overheard him joking about how the squirrel has been trapped and skinned and can now be eaten.

While watching an episode, she decides. While wondering what makes all those images so delicious. The colorful pies that the women with high cheek bones are holding up, the crisp red rooftops of their homes, the shiny clothes, and creamy hair.

Nobody understands my intentions anymore. Now there is nobody who understands my intentions. I only want to fly in and out and between the tall buildings of one large city. There is no more pleasure to be had. I like watching, but it is not pleasurable now that it is all there is to do. I need distraction, but cannot find it. She now knows that without company of some sort one thinks too much and too often. I need religion. I need to believe that I am here for a reason . . . so that I then can go to heaven, where life is like an episode. It is unbearable to exist in any meantime otherwise. It has become unbearable. There must be a truth that is also true for those who have been tortured, falsely imprisoned, those who die young, who live with their diseases, those who have watched their children be killed or their mothers be raped. If there is a truth it must feel true for everybody.

I want to discover that I have a superpower. Strength is pointless, she is not a character on the screen. I could walk around this cold city all night trying to find somebody to save just to come home alone and useless still. Mind control is unnecessary, who would you command? Bring me my order, but she was going to anyway. Love me, they wouldn't know how, you'd have to be very specific every second of every day, which would be too much work. But to fly, to be able to fly in and between these buildings . . . What if you could have the superpower of being able to feel loved, really loved? By everybody I meet? There is no superpower that would help in real life except the power to make people love you. What would invisibility matter if finding crimes to solve or people to rescue requires a life of searching in the cold of winter or heat of summer? What would lasers and beams matter when to win a fight you have to pick a fight? But even if you could fly you would still be flying alone. She has learned from her episodes that to have magic you have to believe in magic. You have to believe, really believe, so much so that if you dove and fell off that cliff you would be shocked because you knew it was impossible. But how many times has that happened already, the shock of knowing what could not happen already has? The shock of falling when you jumped, because you jumped, because you really believed you couldn't fall.

We take from those we love until there is nothing left, not even any of the love itself left over. To not let go after that would be for a spider to carry on its back the desiccated remains of a moth. Loving you made me a tarantula trying to hold the ashes of what was once a caterpillar. Whatever makes us happy, we will want to do again and again, it is that wanting that we believe is love. Until it does not give us pleasure, we will want. You will want. Until every thought of what you can't have . . . it is the waiting for the train to arrive, outside in the night in the cold rain.

Every single thing we make will get thrown away. Everything is already waste. This bed, this table, this glass, this bottle, this desk will be thrown away. This arm, this leg, this hair, this head . . . Everybody once famous will feel either immensely, or a little bit more, alone when nobody applauds anymore. Being intimate with another body can bring ecstasy or repulsion. Nobody wants to know how his father fumbles as a lover. If you fought the man who wronged your wife, it was shameful how you lost, if you didn't fight you're ashamed. You cannot, no matter how much you want to, make a window through a wall with your bare hands, or by banging your head.

It could always be worse. It could be better. You will die. But I am tired of being told to feel happy about how much more others suffer, how much worse suffering can be. You will die. You know what you will lose, but not what you will, or if there is something to, gain.

I want to fly in between tall buildings and see through all the glass, then soar up towards green trees closer to the night sky. But you would still be alone. Death is the only thing you can want and be certain you will have. Death is the only logical thing to let yourself want.

I wish I could always feel like a once blind man on the first day he can see again, I wish I could see for the first time in my life, again and again, every day. I wish that when one lantern went up in the sky to celebrate or mourn and others followed like soldiers or brothers they would eventually disappear or go on up into space rather than eventually falling back down somewhere to be waste, something made somewhere. I wish there was a way to save everything destroyed already. I wish there was some place to go once the body goes. I wish I knew where I will go so I could prefer to keep on living. I wish to be the wind in between tall buildings in one particular city. I want the distraction of being in love, of wanting something so much that I know it must be something I can believe in. Then when it happens, when you have it, you know you can believe in other things you've been waiting to believe in as well. I want an afterlife so much that it must be something I can and should believe in. Why would you need a God or a purpose so you do not suffer if they are not real? I want music to be only one of the ways a heart soars, not the only way. I want what I am doing right now, watching this episode, to be something meaningful to what will happen when I die. I want to know that I will always be, in some way.

I wish I were something that is supposed to be very small like an ant, or something that is supposed to be very large like a whale. I want to not feel shame for being too small, or too big. I want to be something that lines over time but does not show age like the palm of a hand.

You can still love people without ever wanting to be in the same room, you know, without ever seeing them again, or wanting or trusting their company. Every magical thing conceivable might be real. If you were not in this body you could know this. If you did not have your body you could live like people do on an episode on a screen. No wonder you still want to believe in God. On your way to the fieldtrip, who will be the teacher who sits next to you on the bus full of children who do not like you otherwise? Who else would make one eventually have to pick you for their team and let you play?

Why does everything that could be good happen to you when you can't understand it, or know what to do, the right thing to do? Once you can make the most of what has happened to you, when you finally understand, because it's happened, you don't get the chance to do it again, to do it right.

The women on the screen sometimes are lonely too. They say sincere things like "I am lonely, the loneliness is palpable."

Now that I know how to be young without being bad, I am not young anymore. Once you learn how to be old without feeling so alone you will die.

You have lived long enough. I have already lived long enough to know what is and isn't a factual portrayal of most things in an episode. When she sees a dinner table beautifully set with candles she knows that the candle wax will ruin the silk cloth as the candles melt. Scenes where heroes run in snow remind her of how difficult it is, how much harder you work to pull your legs up. When people jump in the sea mouths and eyes open she can taste and feel the sting of the salt. She has fallen enough times to know that jumping off a roof would keep you from getting back up right away, even if you did need to chase.

Remember when we made lists of the birthdays of everybody we had ever kissed, then everybody we had been friends with at school, then every boy we had ever loved who never loved us back, all to see if the stars made human patterns? Remember when we stood in front of each other in front of a mirror naked to confirm what we already were sure of, our bodies were the same shape, only mine was big and yours was small. Remember when you found me crying under covers and you kissed my face through the blankets? Remember when you told me that I will be one of the three people you see in heaven? Remember when you were sad so we stayed up for two nights under covers watching episode after episode? Now I am again the child who nobody wants to play with, I am the one whose intentions are always misunderstood. Without you I will never be the funny one, the good one again, and because of you I know that I never was.

I know that this feeling is why the number six has always been important, why I have wanted six to be at the end of everything. If I wait my life will end, involuntarily, at an age that ends with a seven or an eight instead.

Maybe I will come back as a brown poisonous spider with a red violin on her back, one she can't see, and so doesn't know exists. I know what those dreams I told you about meant now. Maybe I will come back as a snake who slithers away from a snake's egg, then does not need other snakes again.

When she was young she would have dreams that were just a texture, the texture of skin floating right above soft grain, or ever so slightly above the moving face of the ocean. She was afraid, but the pleasure was palpable, overwhelming, and she knew that she would sink in it if she didn't wake up. She will die in the salty ocean. It is destined for her. It is why she could never learn how to swim no matter how many times someone tried to teach her. She can float. How long can someone survive in the dark, cold, ocean if they are only floating? How else would she do it? A gun is not an option. She cannot have whoever finds her first find the blood. Poisons are too risky if her body rejects them to keep her alive, but broken somehow. She will not cut her own skin, slaughtering an animal so she can live, an animal whose pain you can feel. She knows the smell, the heat that comes from the body of a slaughtered animal, she has lived long enough to know that.

His mouth that day tasted and smelled like a slaughtered animal.

I would love to give away all these little things I own now. She has always loved that feeling of having cleaned out and made use of everything. These nightstands will live on. Before I die I would love to go away and eat things without feeling that food is a sweet poison that keeps me alive but makes me too large to love. I would love that time, the last time, when I get to say one last thing that they have to listen to. They will remember whatever it is I write or say now because they will think back and remember that it was the last thing somebody ever said. Even if it's something you have said many times before, now they will remember it. Like, I love you. I really truly loved you. I was wrong, but now do you see how I was right? I apologize. I am sorry. Forgive me. I did not know how to love, perfectly. Everybody I loved I am sure still loves me, and I am sure I still love everybody I have ever said I loved. We just don't speak, or laugh, or touch anymore. All there is in life now is this sticky yellow light in an apartment in a city, then the pasty blue light in an office in a city. And you want a weightless white light.

I know everything there is to know already.

She knows history, enough history to know what will happen to people because of what has already happened to her and others. When people eat or drink on the screen she can imagine what almost everything tastes like. And when a song comes on while they are happy, or when they are sad, or when they are driving away, she usually knows who first sang it. This is how very long she has already lived. She has lived long enough to hear the news of the death of a man who couldn't want her no matter how much she tried. He drank so much that he died in a pool of his own vomit and blood and was found in a bathroom stall by the beautiful woman he had wanted instead of her. She couldn't love more than she already has. It would not be possible. She couldn't love a man more than the one she has wanted the most. She couldn't love a woman more than the one she does not speak to, but still thinks everything to. She couldn't love a child more than the one she held as the child bled. She asked why does the blood scare you and rocked and kissed her head while she heard the muffled, mumbled words "because it is a red monster." I would be mocking myself if I were to moan when another man kissed my neck. If I were to close my eyes slowly, like an antelope does, again while a man kissed. I would be mocking friendship if I ever said I loved a woman again. To say anything to another child would be a lie.

When she watches the people on the screen she understands with her body and memory what they are doing. When she sees people kissing . . . drinking . . . sitting in offices . . . carrying wood . . . raking leaves she knows how the grass pushes back, how it resists and how that makes the rake pull against the arms . . . how uneven the ground and pressure. She knows things about language, how difficult it is to remember, how it is necessary to practice until it becomes physical function or you forget . . . how similar it is to love, practicing love so you know that you love and whom you love. She knows how the skin of the dead feels against her hands . . . love always ends then, even when it doesn't . . . She has lived long enough to know that a woman speaking fondly of her husband's habits to another woman on a train or a bus or a coffee shop is not somebody to be jealous of because even she may be alone too. She knows hate . . . failure . . . guns and how the recoil would always keep her from hitting her target. She has seen six policemen in four cars dragging away one woman sitting in front of a hospital repeating one thing, "They told me I needed it." They told me I needed it. They told me I needed it. They told me I needed it. She knows it is better to buy expensive things that will last longer than to make even more waste. She knows what it is to be the poor and young and even happy and does not want to imagine what it is to be even more old and alone. Already she has started to witness her body adorn itself for death with lines, grooves, markings, frills, and different shades of skin on skin. She already knows why those women on the screen swoon even while kissing men who they know do not love them. At one point she would not have known what a doily was. Now she has lived long enough and learned enough language to know. And to know that someone has taken the smell out of the roses. She knows what roses used to smell like. Real life is not like an episode, even a very good speech in real life does not always get applause. The rich will always need to feel that the poor are finding redemption.

She wants to speak to somebody who loves her, but instead she has plastic bags, and plastic ties, and plastic bowls, and plastic pins.

It is best to have love she knew then, and knows now, accomplishment and goodness are otherwise pointless.

Nothing that already is does then not want to be, it only wants to be good.

It is best to believe the children who have been stolen and imprisoned and raped and robbed and raped and raped again did something to deserve it.

On her skin there is a difference between a white spot, a red spot, and a brown spot. They happen for different reasons. Her eyes look smaller on her face now, her nose and ears do not.

If you are looking up while lying on your back on winter grass the bare trees are just black veins on the skin of the sky.

Sometimes she takes the trash out on very cold nights with just a shirt on so that when she goes back inside she could remember comfort for a little while. She should remember that she has something to be grateful for. She is not suffering as much as others do.

I will come back as a cicada who has buried herself underground for seventeen years, whose life is supposed to be lived buried underground. What was I before to have come back so lonely? A tyrant. An enemy of love. A breathtaking heartbreaker. She wants to be a fearless crime fighter, just like in the episodes, not like anybody in real life. She wants to come back as a fearless crime fighter in the mind of somebody who writes her episodes, where every day is spent driving with and speaking to and eating with and running towards and shooting and yelling at, and then chased, and then thanked by people. And so too busy to be sad or not want to be alone.

I will come back as a centipede in the Amazon who can wait and wait then fly to poison a bat in a cave. What was she in the past that she had to come back to life only to want to die? A giant centipede who waited and waited only to pounce on and drain bats, a spider who couldn't appreciate the perfect red violin on her back, a cicada who resented having to live any of her life not buried underground. She wants to come back as a man, or a woman with hair she can always wear down, somebody strong enough to shoot a gun straight despite the recoil, a person, a body that nobody in the world thinks is undesirable.

All the palm readers have always said she would have two children. Now she knows they might have been referring to the two she wouldn't let live. She must die, she has already outlived her children.

Everybody desperately wants to be loved, either because they have never had love, or because they always have.

If I had all the money in the world I would not be happy, but at least you would feel safe enough to stay alive.

There are four kinds of people in the world. The largest group is here to suffer in their bodies. The second largest is here to live off of and ignore their suffering, even blame them for their suffering. A minority is here to make them suffer. A smaller minority is here to try to keep them from suffering. When you thought you belonged to one group then find out you really belong in another . . . it is always devastating.

The only time she feels men are still good is when on the screen in front of her six of them, tall and proud, carry a coffin; or when they all stand and salute someone powerless in unison.

If only I could find a diamond shaped diamond on the ground on my way home, a diamond so large that I could hardly carry it. You would carry it, drag it, lift it up and fall down with it in your arms over and over again until your spine became misshapen, as long as you made it home with that diamond. Then I could sell it and buy things that would distract me. I would have chefs and drivers to keep me company.

If life went in a line, then so much want would be like living, but it is made up of only small circles, and so much want only takes you back to the end and the beginning.

I have to say over and over again that without you it is a world where there are no large suns, no moons, no planets, only distant constellations, many big things made small and shiny only because they are so very far away.

I have already been held by a man, carried by a man, pushed down by a man, slapped by a man.

The shapes she thought life took have changed. Once life was like a tree, or a mountain, a thing to start at the bottom of and get to the top. Now there are only circles.

Once your own thoughts become things shredding at you minute by minute, knives or razors or shards of glass, what then is there to do? And the biggest shame is that as long as you are alive there is still always a small part of you that thinks you will finally be happy. People will finally understand you, miss you, know that all the bad things they did to you were really bad, once they know you are dead, even if only for one minute.

What does it feel like to be lonely, to be all alone every night? It would surprise you . . . There is a nausea, a panic, as if something is always about to happen and nobody else will be witness, as if she is about to go on stage and speak meaningful words she cannot remember, a dull quiver like nausea, as if she has already spoken and nobody laughed, and nobody applauded.

The opposite of pain is not joy, it is only the lack of pain.

I've always wanted to live inside the corner of a wall, with an arch for a doorway, and inside a bed made of matchboxes. Then you should come back as a storybook mouse. If I only had a son, a daughter to hold in a dark cold corner. Then I would shiver, but I could live only to think about keeping alive this one thing.

I will give away all my organs first, that way I can die knowing I have done something good. What can you give away before you die? Not the ears or the eyes because nobody will take them now. My heart nobody will take, not as long as you are alive. I have one kidney and some of the marrow in my bones to give. Maybe I will befriend the man I keep alive and it will be like something that happens in an episode where by chance people meet people and love them at any age, at any cost . . . Later he will thank me, and ask me to stay a while. I will choose the glass of wine, and as you dreamily stare out his window, he will wish you had asked for coffee instead.

You wouldn't believe what lived in the attic. I was sure it was something mean like a rat, so I was afraid. Other times I knew it must be something kind like a bird, so I was sad. I couldn't tell. But from the sounds that came from the attic . . . It could have been a family of armadillos racing on their spinning backs, or pigeons who have broken their wings dragging them while trying to take off head first again and again against the wall. It could have been anything vicious, or something that suffers. You know, once, a long time ago, for a little while a palm dove hit the glass of her bedroom window every morning. Every morning around the same time she woke up to the thuds of a pinkish gray dove's chest slamming into the glass. But this was only a squirrel. A squirrel who had trees and an attic. It was not mean like a rat. It was not kind like a bird. It was only a squirrel who had an attic, until it was trapped.

EVENING TIME IN THE CITY

You are thinking about him now because you always are. You are watching a movie while you are thinking about him but you are only thinking about him. The thoughts of him leave you open to new ideas new ways to feel better or worse and yes sometimes ways to believe that everything happens as it should. What happens in a movie can come to mean a lot to you. You shouldn't be ashamed of this. Somebody is falling in love in this movie and love is love wherever it is found. And this seems to be real love but they are still so young. This makes you feel better they are young still, they don't know they will fail. The man is a good man and the woman is a good woman. This makes you feel bad because it may mean they deserve each other and will end up happy even after the movie ends. Don't worry. You want to hate them because you are waiting for him to love you. You want love too. You want him to love you. Think about how young they are how everything will change once they get to know each other better. If they are together now soon they will not be because people change everything changes. You may be too old for love now. They are young. They met each other before they knew that nothing stays the same. There is probably another woman who is watching the same movie right now somewhere far away who is with somebody who she knows she will never leave. Unlike you she thinks that if she were free true love would find her. This woman thinks it is possible to find love because her lack of love does not make it impossible. You know that a person can be alone every day of their life waiting and never find true love. Her life is not proof of anything but yours may be. She did not find love because she found something else instead but you just have nothing. Don't worry about what you said because nothing is good so nothing you can say is really that bad. You think you cannot appreciate this young couple's love only because you are mature and it is a movie and because you are mature you know how things change. Even though you are waiting for a man who doesn't want you who is not a good man who you most likely would not want anyway if he did want you. You want him to want you. You want to feel something for somebody and have them feel it back for you. Because nobody ever has. Felt something for you. You want somebody to. People in movies wait for love too. But you do not wait with a life that flashes by in scenes. You wait with the slippery weight on your chest. The air you take in goes down too far all the way to your gut and slowly sputters out. You wait because he makes you feel bad about yourself. It is easier to wait your whole life in a movie because twenty years can just fly by in a scene here a scene there. It is easier to be happy in the meantime. It is harder in real life to wait for love your whole life. And it is always your whole life you've lived every day. In the movie the young man in love is often found speaking to other men. When he is speaking to other men everything is so simple because they have their own language. You think about this because the man you are waiting to love you makes you feel that he would rather be around other men than be around you. You want to believe that it is only because everything is so simple and good when he is around other men. You study these scenes because you want to know what can make men want to be around women as much as they want to be around other men. You really want to know what would make him want you but you put it on all men having a language because that makes you feel better. As you watch the movie you notice that other than simple nuances in ways of expressing physical affection conversations between the men and the women are similar. You can imagine this man saying most of the things he says to the male characters to the woman he loves but he touches her differently. Conversations are not very different. This makes you wonder what the real difference is because obviously there is a difference. Does he want a woman to touch him? He does not seem to really want that because he knows you would give it to him if he wanted it but he does not take it. It hurts you that he doesn't want you. It makes you sad. You must try to be completely natural when you speak. Completely yourself so that you are the most masculine you can be. That is the only way to be like a man and have men want to be around you. By being your most true self you become more human. In that way that human way everybody is the same you can become most like a man. Then men will want to be around you. There should be nothing excessive and so unnecessary about what you say and do. Then you will be more like a man and he will want to talk to you. Everything is so simple. He loves her because he has not yet heard her thoughts. Her little petty ignorant jumbled unpunctuated thoughts. He just sees her actions every now and again from scene to scene. You have had some negative thoughts about him. Does that mean you deserve to live without love? People in love in movies also have negative thoughts about each other, they just can't hear them. You have thought he is too short and he will be completely bald soon. You have imagined how his being so short could be disappointing. The young man that the young girl loves jumps off a cliff and into the water. His body is beautiful to you as you watch not only because it is supposed to be. He is not supposed to repulse you but he is not supposed to be as beautiful as he becomes to you in this scene. He is as beautiful as the cliff of rock and the sun and the rushing waters. Suddenly he becomes excessively beautiful to you. Why you ask yourself is his body so beautiful. The hair on his body makes it so the strength of the legs and arms and chest is not ornate or diluted by smoothness. The lack of breasts makes it so the chest is one formidable flat surface not carrying loose ends that do not belong to it. His body is beautiful. You want one like it near yours. He leans in and says to a woman in a whisper I will stay here all night if you want. I can wait here all night. His body is a strong long suffering thing. You are not good looking really not to most people probably but you had hoped he would find you beautiful. He has said certain things that made you think he finds you beautiful. You suddenly feel that if he were to know this waitress from this scene in the movie he would think that she is a better woman than you are. He would want to talk to her. The waitress is his type and you aren't. You feel inferior to the waitress. She is smart but not a book smart with a very open sexiness. What could she have been other than a waitress. She doesn't even think about stuff like that. She lives in her beautiful body. She practically lives off of the land in this small town and she is beautiful and she cannot escape from the people she knows who know her and this makes her real and strong since she has never run away or wanted anything better because she has had to deal with people and so takes everything with a grain of salt. She dances whenever she feels like it. That's not how things work in real life. It's not that easy to dance whenever you want because people start staring at you and you begin to feel bad. But she probably knows about football and other games and she probably says the right thing when she is with all his friends to make them laugh and make him proud he is with her in front of them. She likes to sing. She could not write anything herself. But somebody has to write songs for people like her to sing. This is a good movie. He would like this movie. He sees himself as somebody who likes being in nature. He really likes movies and books about people who live off of or are close to the land. Why does he not like you? In movies women and men don't have to really talk about themselves. You see everything important that happened to them and everything brave they have done in scenes. They stay so humble and so concise. Whether they are good or bad they are not that awkward type of arrogant that comes from having to talk about yourself. This makes the kind ones seem even kinder and the cruel ones seem smoother less clumsy. If they have traveled you see them having traveled you don't have to hear about all the places they have been. You just see scenes of them walking on different types of land behind different types of scenery so you can respect them for having done things instead of wondering what they are doing and why they are telling you what they are telling you? What do they want for you to think about them? What are you supposed to feel about them now that you have heard these things? You told him once about how you've been to every restaurant in the city. He said no, you haven't. All of a character's horrible memories can be told in flashbacks or in very simple sentences they speak despite themselves so the person who is supposed to love them can respect them for what they have survived without wondering why they are speaking for so long. When somebody says I had a horrible childhood or hard life or worked hard to get a job you just can't ever know what they mean. And when they tell you stories to highlight and explain they may be lying or speaking for too long. What do you want me to do or think of you right now? Here you can just see her parents being mean to her and you can respect her for that because she isn't telling you so isn't asking you for anything. People want to tell you what happened to them so you know them because they want you to know them because they want to know themselves and they won't know themselves until somebody they think something of tells them what they think of them. Then someday when they are sad they want you to say oh you are very good and brave remember that time you did that thing you told me you did? Maybe it is only you who wants this? You told him things but he didn't ask any questions and he doesn't remember.

BUSES

Well, he got kicked out of their apartment and had to send the kid to live with his mother now she is gone and he is gone. But he was so nice to you. He seemed very kind. He was good to her too obviously. When she called and he picked up and he said Baby, why did you do it? Baby? That's when you knew he wasn't lying, he had had his own dialogue then. Why would he lie on a bus to a stranger? He called her Baby even though he told you he was done with her and wouldn't talk to her anymore. That's how you know someone is telling the truth when they can't stop lying right in front of you. What right did you have to be scared for him? People who say they are done with somebody and then call that somebody Baby are a dime a dozen. Eventually the one to your right became Mr. Right. He said, I thought I was her Mr.

Right. He would not even have let his ex-girlfriend go with him on trips because he didn't like her having to be on long bus rides like this. He would not bring a woman here, this is not where a Ms. Right belongs. This man says this like a good father dreams a good man would say things so some men do want some things to be like what good fathers say they should be for their daughters. Mr. Right and you were not so close though. Not as close as the guy who called his drug addicted ex girlfriend Baby. You are glad that lady who was calling her baby a fucking asshole got off on the last stop. It's not good when you see a baby being handled roughly and called an asshole and don't do anything. Where are you going to hide her baby from his mother on a bus though? Stop the bus! This lady is crazy and is shaking her baby and calling the baby an asshole. But everybody heard her already, and heard the baby. At night the rap artist is trying to put his hands inside your shirt and you're so cold at night here with the air conditioner always on on the bus. You think you will let him because he was nice in some ways when we were talking earlier and very openly about how he just got out of prison. And you opened your big mouth and started talking about things to do with fucking this other guy you had just come from being with. But he was nice then. For example, when he told you that people were made when death fucked life. And when he told you he read a lot in prison. You wrote something down about death fucking life and thought maybe life is all about writing things down so this ride is worth it in the end if you leave with more things written down. Those boys who said they were carrying guns who insisted the bus driver was racist and kept calling him a nigger and wanted to shoot him when you all had to get off were not so scary because you were really tired at that point when all the Mexicans left and the white people with many children got on right around. But when they harassed the girl with track marks on her arms because she said she was horny and this man she just came back from seeing wanted nothing to do with her . . . that was uncalled for. You would have said something about it but she was pretending to be enjoying the attention and you didn't think she would protect you if they had tried to hurt you because you were trying to protect her. You know the man who thought Jews owned the world and that's why there is a small k on potato chips to indicate that they're kosher would not have tried to save you because he taught you a lot about good and bad pussy as apparently in other parts of the world women are more likely to have sex with him without being all weird about it. He was very upset that often he has had to buy bitches shit and because Jews controlled foods and the best day of his life was when he met his weight lifting idol eating outside a gym . . .

THINGS THAT HAPPEN TO CHILDREN IN THE CITY

This poor little girl. By the time we got here it was too late. This poor little girl under these lights, all cut up and bloody on the concrete. God only knows what they have done to her. Even now she's still screaming and crying, so upset that she's shaking and mumbling. It probably doesn't help, all of us staring at the same time. People trying to put their hands on her shaking head. She just keeps on shivering and mumbling, trying to slap hands off her head. I wonder who she would go to though, if she had to reach for one of us, which one of us it would be. The crazy thing, as wild as she is acting, might try and hold on to Ida. Ida. Everybody thinks Ida is so wonderful. Everybody loves Ida. I don't know what the hell for. The one time I turned to her for help she listened for a while with that half smirk half grin on her face, then said something like I don't want to get involved, and something else about every story having two sides. What kind of thing is that to say to someone who is hurting and turns to you for help? It's not like I had ever asked her for anything before. I usually am the one people turn to for help. I hardly ever turn to them for anything. Of course, she couldn't just be the bitch she is and say flat out what she was thinking. I don't care about you, so, shut the hell up and quit your whining. That's how she made me feel though. She had to mask it with her fancy talk about not wanting to make me feel this way, or that way, but she just thinks this is, and that is, so on and so forth. Whatever she said. She's always got something to say about her goddamn boundaries. Or her space, or something else about what she needs to do for herself. The bitch said that if you really love somebody you want them to be happy, even when they leave you and you still love them, because you loved them and not what they did for you. She got that from one of her self-help books. If you really love somebody and they have already left you, then you can't help but imagine them hurting too. You scream at the sky as if your organs have been ripped out of you or something. She can't be human for one second though. There were times I felt I loved him so much I wanted to pretend I was dying so he wouldn't be afraid of being with me forever, for a long time. He could feel like he just had to be good to me for a little while longer and then it would all be over. I feel like I am dying anyway. Ida would say something about how we all are, we all die alone. She said stupid shit about how I will find somebody if I love myself first and that people shouldn't need each other, they should want each other, and that's how life is. What does she think I think life is? I loved him. I really loved him. I loved sitting next to this person who I knew and slept next to and could reach for when I wanted. I had a person sitting there next to me on Ida's couch once, my person, so I didn't have to feel alone while in a room with Ida. I wanted this person so much I must have needed him. You want something like that unless you need it. He knew me, to everyone else I was a stranger. I am a stranger now to everyone. Looking at Ida's face reminds me that without him everyone has the power to make me feel like she makes me feel. It reminds me of one of those future world stories about worlds where all the books have been burned or where people aren't supposed to feel things except what they're told to feel. The main character is always too afraid to admit to anyone that they have a book or a feeling or somebody will report them. You have to find out who those very few people are, the ones who are secretly like-minded, so you can say anything that's on your mind at all. I walk around and I can't speak because I don't trust anybody to not judge me. Turn me into the others by telling them I'm crazy. She's probably already told everybody the thing I said about how I've been feeling since he left me. She probably already mocked me using her psycho babble. I don't know, maybe she doesn't try to be unkind, maybe she would like it if people treated her this way, so that's how she treats people. She gave me that stupid book that talked about grief and making what you want just happen in life. Everything is a blessing and someday you will know why. It said some other stuff too about not caring what the outcomes are as long as you care about your own actions or something. But if you are not supposed to care if anything actually happens or not, why would you care about your actions in the first place? Be detached from your desires it said, but imagine exactly what you want so it happens, at the same time. But if you really want something you should let go and just focus on the present. Every situation is the seed of opportunity, but you have to pretend you don't want anything now. I don't get that mumbo jumbo. You have to want without wanting and feel without feeling. I'll always be stuck in a room with people like Ida who look down at me, or sometimes just look through me. I always knew when he would laugh, I always knew what to say to make him laugh. But everybody loves and respects Ida. This poor little girl is probably in no mind to judge anyway. She wouldn't be able to tell in her condition who is and isn't really going to hurt her again. If she turns to me I will hold on to her until she lets go first. I'm not the kind of person who would tell somebody that I can't hold them anymore, because of my boundaries or whatever else. Not when they are hurting like this. This poor little girl isn't going to turn and hold on to anybody anyway. She just keeps on shaking and fussing. They have to come get her. That's how people lose their minds. You have enough sense to stop trying to reach for people or believe that if you let them put their hands on you they would keep them there, so you just shake alone and can't ever stop.

CPSIA information can be obtained
at www.ICGtesting.com
Printed in the USA
FFOW02n2028070718
47352569-50399FF